THE COWBOY'S ONE AND ONLY

THE BROTHERS OF THATCHER RANCH - BOOK 1

APRIL MURDOCK

CONTENTS

APRIL MURDOCK	*The Cowboy's One and Only*	
Prologue		3
Chapter 1		5
Chapter 2		13
Chapter 3		17
Chapter 4		25
Chapter 5		33
Chapter 6		45
Chapter 7		49
Chapter 8		61
Chapter 9		75
Chapter 10		81
Chapter 11		85
Chapter 12		97
Chapter 13		107
Chapter 14		119
Chapter 15		133
Chapter 16		137
Chapter 17		141
Chapter 18		145
Chapter 19		147
Chapter 20		153
Chapter 21		161
Chapter 22		165
Chapter 23		175
Epilogue		179
APRIL MURDOCK	*Preview - The Billionaire's High School Reunion*	
	Chapter 1	193

Want a Free Book?	203
About April Murdock	205

Copyright © 2020 April Murdock and Sweet River Publishing

All rights reserved.

No part of this book may be reproduced in any form or by any electronic or mechanical means, including information storage and retrieval systems. Publisher expressly prohibits any form of reproduction.

∼

This is a work of fiction. Any references to names, characters, organizations, places, events, or incidents are either products of the author's imagination or are used fictitiously.

THE COWBOY'S ONE AND ONLY

THE BROTHERS OF THATCHER RANCH - BOOK 1

APRIL MURDOCK

PROLOGUE

Logan

Seeing *her* was a spike of clarity straight into his veins, a combination of hot and cold overcoming him as his gaze drank her in.

Her hair the same intensity as red swirls of the wild strawberry jam he put on his toast every morning, eyes so blue, they must have taken the sky's pigment for themselves.

Lips curled into a sly, beam as if she knew something that Logan didn't and oh, how he wanted to know.

She sat with her legs swinging haphazardly, leaning forward just enough to make him question what she was doing there—was she about to say hello or spring to her feet and walk away without a word?

Seeing her brought him back to a place he'd never been.

Yet there they were…

CHAPTER 1

Logan
One Day Earlier

Almost.

Logan sucked in air through his nostrils as he felt his right bicep shuddering, failing. He gripped hard onto the rock with the slightly curved toes of his climbing shoes, swinging his other hand to the pencil thin handhold—just as his first hand lost its grip.

His entire body shook with the effort. Above, the next handhold was a long lunge away. If he missed it…

Quickly, he shook off the thought. There was no room for missing it. Logan semi-ducked into a near crouch, launched his body up and—

Got it!

The impact nearly winding him, Logan scrambled up and over to safety. On all fours, he caught he paused for a moment to catch his breath. Adrenaline ripped through him and his eyes traveled downward to take in the scene below.

Would you look at that! That's why I do this. This makes it all worthwhile.

Staring off into the expanse, he felt indestructible, exhilarated.

Hundreds of feet below him was Sagebrush Texan ground or as Logan called it, "reality".

With only a Petzl harness, belay, and double pulley, Logan had climbed the sheer rock face. He had summited the first mountain of the Potest range.

He'd been practicing for months, just to conquer the harrowing pass and now, he'd finally done it.

Logan spread his limbs and reclined onto his back, letting the mountain air lap coolness on his body. It was much cleaner up there, away from the emissions of below.

Overhead, the sky was a striking teal, the shade reserved for Photoshopped advertisements of Bahamas resorts.

Logan found himself wondering what the sky would ask if it could talk.

Is it asking me when I'm heading back down?

The reality that scraped at the edges of his consciousness were still gratefully out of range, even with the thought, at least for the time being.

Logan turned his head slightly so he could toss a glance down again, toward the speck that was his home. With the distance and range between them, it seemed abstract, insubstantial.

If Logan kept climbing and never looked back, or just climbed down another side of the Potest range, kept walking wherever his legs took him, he'd never have to go back. *That* reality would cease to exist for him

It would be that easy.

Logan shut his eye, blocking out the speck, even as he knew in no way would it be that easy. He'd never be able to just walk away.

As much as he wanted to, every time he came out here to the mountain range and tested and battled and conquered himself against the infallible rocky indifference, he knew.

He'd have to go back home, sooner or later.

He had responsibilities.

Almost on cue, a voice crackled nearby.

"...looo! Hel-lo?"

It took Logan a few seconds to clue in that it was his walkie-talkie coming alive to life in the pocket of his cargo pants. Stifling a sigh, he took it out in time to hear the question.

"What the heck, Logan?" the disembodied voice demanded again.

Logan reclined back and lay there for a few more seconds, inhaling the mountain air, eyeing the shimmering mountain-bordered sky, as if he could stay like this forever.

Abruptly, he sat up, the sweet reverie shattering. Reality was calling after all.

He pressed the walkie-talkie talk button and spoke in a rush of breath.

"Coming."

Shoving the device back in his pocket, he ambled to his feet and began the descent down the mountain. The radio buzzed a few times, no doubt another brother reaming him out, but Logan didn't care. They'd got what they wanted already. He was on his way home.

This was exactly the reason he didn't like bringing the walkie-talkie with him on climbs. Being tethered to home with an electronic box that could buzz to life anytime was not his idea of freedom. Yet his mother wouldn't allow him to leave without it and it saved him from having to listen to his brothers' endless complaints so the walkie came, despite Logan's inner annoyance.

Logan forced his mind off that and trained his focus on the sights around him.

The way down was never what it was going up. It had a different allure, details no one noticed on the ascent; a chance pool of crystalline water, a scissor-tailed flycatcher eyeing him with an alert carefulness as she perched on her stick-jabbing nest, a curving sit-worthy Southern oak.

But Logan wouldn't get to enjoy that, not this time. He'd have to go fast, too fast to notice anything other than where the next foothold or handhold would be.

His brothers were waiting and they didn't like waiting. The longer they anticipated Logan , the louder they'd complain. He knew it was better to get down there and get this thing over with.

Logan spotted them long before he was in their earshot. Chance and Chase's twin dark heads leaned against the side of the rock as they passed a plastic bag of something back and forth, Garrett's muscular form standing to the side, his blond head craned up to watch as Logan scrambled down.

Only when Logan's foot touched down on the soft mash grass, did Chance salute him with mock respect.

"Nice of you to grace us with your presence."

Chase smiled to indicate he wasn't overly annoyed, popping a gummy bear into his mouth and Logan suddenly realized what had been in the plastic bag. It struck him funny that his tough, cowboy brothers were sharing a bag of gummy bears. Before he could laugh out loud at them, Garrett strode over to Logan.

"Listen, I know you don't like this anymore than we do, but you can't just do that, okay?" Garrett grumbled. Leftover adrenaline thrummed through Logan's veins. His brother was right. He didn't want to do this but there he was, swallowing his words as he took off his climbing gear and let words float stagnantly in the air between them.

He wanted to walk, to move. He wanted to do anything but *this.*

Garrett grabbed his forearm.

"Hey, you hear me? You can't just go running up the rock wall like that."

"Hey, lay off, Garrett." Chase waved Garrett away with his tan cowboy hat before replacing it on his head.

Always the peacemaker, Chase has to be, Logan thought.

"I'm sorry, man," Logan mumbled, not meeting his brother's eye. "I just wanted to think."

Liar, a little voice taunted him. If anything, that was the problem—*overthinking* was what he wanted to escape.

"Think about what?" Garrett let go, used the hand to rake through his short blond hair. "It's happening, whether we like it or not."

"I know," Logan sighed.

"This is terribly touching and all." Chance jumped to his feet, digging into the almost empty plastic bag to grab the last few gummy bears. "But the gummies are as good as gone, and I got bored of this an hour ago."

Chase snorted as he grabbed the bag and looked inside with a raised eyebrow.

"You were practicing on Jim Shoulders an hour ago."

"Hey!" Chance grabbed for it back, but he was too late. Chase was grinning as he popped the last of the candies into his mouth.

Garrett had already stalked away toward the house, shoulders tense. Logan lagged behind, but his oldest brother still addressed him.

"You know she's been planning this for years. Before we were even born."

Logan didn't respond. Garrett would keep on talking, either way, regardless of what Logan said.

"It would be selfish to try and stop her. To keep her here just for us. We're dang grown men, Logey."

That nickname...

Logan's upper lip curled with disgust. The moniker had been one of Chance's lingering gifts to him. When Logan was young, he'd spoken slowly and drawling, like Yogi bear. Chance had dubbed Logan, "Logey Bear". The name and it had stuck—with his whole family, the school kids, and, in the end, all of Sagebrush.

"Are you even listening to me?" Garrett stopped walking, swung him a simmering look, daring him to not respond again.

"Yeah, I am." Logan glared back at him. "And I know, I get it. I'd never try to stop her. I want her to be happy as much as the rest of you."

Garrett shoved his hands in his blue jean jacket pockets and continued walking.

"Then why in the heck—when she's about to sit down and tell us the details—did you wander off all the way to your precious mountain and…"

The rest of what he said blurred away in Logan's mind. Ma called it his "defense mechanism", how a haze settled over Logan's mind in times like those. He didn't know what it was, only that when things got to be too much, he tuned it out. He didn't do it on purpose, necessarily, it was just how things worked.

Ever since *that* day, at least.

"Dang it, Logan! Don't you go off on me!" Garrett's voice pierced through, drawing him back to the present. Behind them, Chance whistled low and chuckled, while Chase muttered something that sounded like, "Come on now, boys."

"Right, I get it, she's going," Logan snapped at Garrett. "Just wanted to put it off, I guess. Is that so hard to understand?"

He stormed the rest of the way to the ranch, his climbing shoes smashing so hard into the dew-wet dirt that they stuck in places. Normally, the sight of the red stone and white gables filled him with warmth. The same with the spread of blooming gardens in front of it and beyond, the rolling hills and their thick sage scent.

But now, it only registered as a pit in his stomach, a settling of something into some airless, lightless place.

Yes, there would be no putting this off anymore.

It was truly back to reality.

CHAPTER 2

Frankie

"For Pete's sake, Frances Eileen Mills, you get back here this instant!"

Halfway into the barn, Frankie froze and groaned inwardly.

He caught me!

"Elmer," she breathed.

"Don't you Elmer me. I ain't no friend of yours, It's *Uncle Elmer* to you."

Frankie ground her teeth and tried again.

"*Uncle* Elmer, Gus—"

"I don't give a dang what you named that ugly stray cat."

"But he's hungry."

"And feeding it ain't gonna get you nothin' but a beatin'."

Frankie sighed as she straightened her body and brought proffered hand back toward her, ducking the piece of bacon behind her back. Uncle Elmer wasn't serious about a beating, but she still didn't want him riled up. His temper was infamous, even in her household, back in Richmond.

She'd been there less than a week, and their daily quarrels ranged from her sock choices to her feeding the stray cat she'd found a few days ago. Each squabble was starting to wear on her nerves, leaving Frankie feeling like she couldn't do anything right in her uncle's eyes.

"Look at me when I'm talkin' to you, girl!" Elmer insisted.

Frankie eyed Uncle Elmer's face, studying it as if for the first time. His features were wrinkled with set-in rage, pierced with two heavy-lidded warnings for eyes, and riddled with a furious flush from where his chin disappeared into his Santa beard all the way up to his ever-shiny bald head.

To Frankie, he looked as forbidding as ever.

He's all bark and no bite, she reminded herself but it was hard to believe it with flames shooting from his eyes. He put his oversized hands on his hips and glowered mercilessly, his diatribe not concluded.

"You're in my house, so you'll go by my rules. And that's that."

"The cat will die if I don't feed him something. I just can't leave him here hungry," Frankie insisted.

Uncle Elmer shook his head sternly, then raised his squint to the sky in an imploring expression.

"You ain't never gonna make it on this ranch if you mope about thinkin' like that. This ain't Heaven, where every little useless critter is gonna be spared in pairs. Naw. If that cat was gonna die, then you best be letting it go on in peace. And not feeding it my hard-made bacon, and having it muck about scaring my chickens and Raoul."

"Raoul is in fine enough form to stand up for himself," Frankie argued. As if to support her words, the fat rooster strutted through between them with a caw, its head at its usual cocky angle.

Uncle Elmer shook his head again.

"Not on my land and not with my food."

"Fine." Frankie paused, mulling it over. She considered her options. There had to be some way around this, some way to make this work and if there was a loophole, Frankie was certain she'd find it. "So, your rule is that I can't feed Gus on your land, with your food?"

Uncle Elmer squinted at her harder as his beefy right hand reached up to poke his thumb behind his forest green suspenders. He was clearly trying to work out whether she was tricking him with what he liked to call "fancy doily word-play".

"That's the short and tall of it," he finally conceded.

"All right." Frankie went over to him, popping the bacon in her mouth. Gus would have to wait, but she had a plan. "Fair enough."

Uncle Elmer marched after her.

"Now don't you go tryin' to trick me, girl. I was rooting out tricks and tricksters when you were just a fear in the back of your momma's mind."

Frankie rolled her eyes. She knew he didn't mean to hurt her feelings, that his brusque nature was just how he was but still his words stung her if only a little.

I wonder if he knows too.

"You want me to help you feed the pigs or not?" Frankie asked, shoving the thought of her parents out of her head.

"Seein' as that's what was promised, with you comin' out here and all, you dang bet your cushion-loving behind I do."

Frankie trailed behind the older man to the main ranch, keeping her gaze on the wooden three-story with its peeling white paint so she wouldn't look back plaintively for the multi-colored cat.

Little Gus would be fine for the next few hours.
But don't worry, sweet kitty. I'll be back.

CHAPTER 3

Logan

Ma was already there, seated like a queen in her kingdom which doubled as the parlor. Sitting beneath the seemingly unending mass of her favorite colorful afghan, she smoothed the gathers out over her lap. A line of different-sized teacups sat on the table in front of her all filled to the brim with tea steaming the familiar apple cinnamon scent through the room. The sight of them sent a shiver of apprehension through Logan but he refocused his attention on his mother.

It hurt Logan to look at her too.

It wasn't that she was difficult to look at with her unruly silvery taupe curls. The faded blue eyes and snub of a nose always reminded Logan of a pixie. Her rosebud flashed at him to offer him a quick, forgiving smile as always. There was a birdlike awkwardness about her that turned to grace in certain lights.

She brushed a stray lock away from her eyes, just the casual way she always did.

"You found him." Her voice was mellifluous and calm.

She's not angry.

Logan could count on one hand the number of times he'd seen Ma genuinely angry.

"Climbing," Chance said, making a pfft sound, as, in one smooth motion, he slung himself on the couch and under the afghan. "What a surprise."

Garrett dropped to the couch on Ma's other side, scowling.

"Maybe not a shock, but his timing could have been better."

Ma sipped at her tea daintily, nodded sagely.

"Perhaps. But he's here now. You all are. My boys."

Chase plopped on the couch too, taking his tea like a good boy. Logan did the same. There was no use putting it off anymore. He'd prolonged it as long as he possibly could.

The air was pregnant, waiting. Sweetness wafted through the air, with apple cinnamon—and not just the tea. That was Ma's smell too—apples and warmth and all things good.

It smells like home.

"As you all know," Ma began brightly, her voice wobbling not long after she began, "Your father's passing…"

Was unexpected. Unfair. Untimely. Horrible. Lucky…?

A litany of adjectives flew through Logan's mind to describe it but he wisely kept his mouth closed, knowing it was just as hard for her to talk about it as it was for him and his brothers to hear it.

Ma gave her head a little shake, like she was trying to set herself on a more confident path. She cleared her throat before continuing on.

"It's been hard on all of us. On me. I've…" She lifted her tea to her lips but didn't turn the cup back to sip. "Found it hard to keep on going with the way things were. I've been thinking about change, about things I wanted to do. These are things I've wanted for years, way back, before all of you, even before I met your father."

She kept talking, but Logan barely heard her, his mind automatically filtering out what he already knew.

He'd known the day Pa's bloodshot eyes shut for the last time that something intrinsic had broken in their family, that the invisible chain holding things into place had snapped.

He'd known when Ma started forgetting things. When Mary-Ellen showed up, Ziploc bag of chocolate chip cookie dough ready to bake, and Ma had no recollection of inviting her over. He's suspected when the chicken casserole burned in the oven because she'd gone out to the back garden to pick tomatoes and had forgotten about it.

Logan had known when she'd cocooned herself behind her bedroom door for hours, finally emerging with the rarefied air of having returned from a wonderful faraway place. She hadn't even bothered putting the old antique globe or the creased Eyewitness guides back in their normal closet cubby, closer to the end.

It had been a family joke in his youth.

Santa brought second-hand toys for the kids, Happy Foot socks for Pa, and *Eyewitness* guidebooks for Ma. Her little impossible dream she'd called it. She loved living vicariously through the pages and she never missed a single word.

She'd had piles and piles of them through the years. *DK Eyewitness Italy* was one of her favorites. The pages held such delectable close-ups of spaghetti Bolognese and square pizza made with fresh mozzarella that Logan's mouth watered the one time he snuck a look at it.

DK Eyewitness Thailand boasted temple photos of such astonishing beauty it was hard to believe such a place existed. The prices shown in the book were wildly low for some of the local activities and Logan and his brothers had scoffed. But later, when they jested with her about it a Google search proved that the prices were accurate. Then they had laughed about the steal of a travel deal.

There were countless issues in stacks showing all she'd missed by not traveling to London, Los Angeles, Paris, and other ends of the Earth.

Two months before, Pa died and everything had shattered. The defining lines of life as they knew it were destroyed.

And here we are, waiting for what comes next. Except I know what comes next and I don't like it.

Logan caught snatches of what his mother was saying, the fog over his mind was too thick.

"…and Mary-Ellen will be joining me in Rome. You won't believe how she squealed when I told her I was finally, really, *honestly* going to do it. Ah, we danced down around her porch like girls and terrified old Mrs. Barley and a few of her cats too. For a small part I'll be alone, and I'm nervous, but excited too because… well, I need to do this. I've dreamed of seeing the world my whole life. I've only packed what I know I'll need and a few essentials so I won't be weighed down. By anything."

Her smile was different than Logan ever remember it being.

It was wholly her own. It wasn't tinged with anything to dampen it; not guilt, not fear, not longing, or resignation. She was suddenly herself, Cora Thatcher. Not a mother, wife and rancher. She was Cora Thatcher…whoever that might be beyond the constraints of the life she'd always known.

Logan ripped his gaze away. He didn't need to see her like that to know that he was a bad son for feeling how he did. He should be happier for her and he knew it. It was obvious that Ma needed this. More than anything, she deserved it.

One set of words broke through his haze and he looked up suddenly aware of what was going on around him.

"There's one more thing I have to tell you," Ma said slowly, her gaze trailing along the room. Her sons stared at her with expectancy. "Um… I haven't set a return date yet."

Logan felt a shiver of alarm but before he could voice his argument, Garrett interjected.

"Oh, well…" Garrett said.

Ma laughed—an odd, vaulted sound.

"I know how it sounds. But of course I'll come back at some point. I'll miss you like crazy, and you're of course welcome to come along for any part of this trip."

Logan's hands tensed on his tabby cat head-shaped mug.

Well that was a big lie. Welcome? Now that's funny.

Their mother knew as well as they did that her sons couldn't possibly join her in part or at all.

Garrett had to look after the ranch for the family and the twins were deep into their rodeo lives. With the job Logan had recently lost and the climbing gear he'd bought, he didn't exactly have piles of cash available for a vacation.

But she's banking on that too, Logan thought with uncharacteristic bitterness.

"Oh, gosh. I'm sorry." Suddenly, all the easy gaiety dissipated from their mother's voice. Her oval face seemed to sag before them, her tiny hands wilted to the table, releasing the mug. Satisfaction stabbed through Logan as he realized she was having second thoughts. Immediately, his smugness was replaced by shame.

"I know this will be hard on you boys, and… part of me feels like I shouldn't be going. I worry that I shouldn't be leaving you at all."

"Don't say that," Chase interrupted. "You've been a wonderful mother, and you've more than earned some time to yourself. Especially after what happened…"

Chance gave an assured nod, conceding what his twin had said.

"Honestly Ma, you need to do this. *Go*. We're big boys. Adults. We can look after ourselves."

"And I'll make sure the ranch is kept up good and running, don't worry about that," Garrett said. "We'll miss you a ton, but Ma, you've been looking after us for more than thirty years. It's time you look after yourself. And if that means trekking across the planet, then you do that."

He gave the globe a creaky spin as he forced a chuckle.

Ma's gaze moved on to Logan, along with the others.

Your cue, Logan, he thought, reading their expressions clearly.

He knew what his lines were, his part to play, just as well as he knew that he hated it. It was a lie, what he was about to say. Logan couldn't look at her as he spoke and instead shifted his eyes away, not wanting her to read his true feelings in his face.

"They're right, Ma. You deserve it. Go and see the world. I want you to go."

He couldn't look at her after the words were out either. He itched for the outdoors, fresh air, moving, giving vent to the anxious storm brewing in his chest.

It wasn't a complete lie, Logan reasoned to himself. Of course Ma deserved her trip and his brothers were right that they were grown men, that they'd be fine. He found himself wondering if he wasn't being completely selfish for wanting her to stay.

Yep. You're being completely selfish, he confirmed to himself.

Ma had clasped her hands together tightly and put on a valiant smile.

"I know this is going to be hard but I think it will turn out for the best. Each of you needs to finally stand on your own two feet."

Logan could feel her gaze stopping on him but he didn't look up. He wasn't sure if he couldn't or wouldn't.

"Standing?" Chance laughed as he grabbed Chase's cowboy hat off his head and gave it a toss. "Me and Chase are gonna be *riding*. Yee-haw!"

Logan caught her thin smile out of the corner of his eye and watched through his peripheral vision as she spoke again.

"I'm sorry I'll miss so much of that. Your competition's in what? Six months now?" Ma asked.

"Six and a half," Chase confirmed with a grin as he nudged Chance. "Which means we best be training every waking minute."

Chance slapped both his thighs with open palms, gaze already darting outside.

"What d'you reckon I was doing before you busted in making us go on a wild Logey goose chase?"

Garrett rose.

"You need help with anything, Ma?"

She leaned forward but remained in her seat.

"No, I don't think so." She jerked her head so a silvery curl was thrown back. "I've been packing and repacking for a few days. I almost forgot one of the most important details. My flight's in two days."

Two. Days.

"Whoa, that's fast." Garrett moved to hug her.

"Congrats, Ma!" Chance romped over to join the hug, giving her bushy head a pat too. "Maybe you can watch the Houston Livestock Show and Rodeo online, in Cambodia or wherever crazy place you'll be."

Chase was next, smiling broadly.

"I'm sure Ma'll have better things to do than watch you lose."

Everyone laughed, except Logan and Chance, who was puffed up with a frown.

"Watch me beat you, you mean."

All of them, still huddled in a group hug, glanced Logan's way curiously. They silently willed him into the mass.

His body went through the motions—turned-up mouth corners, lifted then descended arms around others, full hug. In his head, he counted to three before releasing his grip.

"You okay?" Ma whispered to him just as he was about to break away.

He stayed rigid.

Why did she have to ask questions she didn't want the answers to?

"I'm fine," he replied quickly, turning away. Ma held him in place with a wispy arm and he paused to struggle against her.

"Want to talk?" she asked softly. This time, with one swift jolt, he was free.

"Maybe later," he said, already headed out of the room.

That's another lie.

He knew all too well what talking would be. More of the same. Talking around all the real issues, swapping lies with an ease they'd gained back in the bad old days.

As much as Logan wanted to reassure Ma some more, savor his last day few days with her, he was tired. His soul was exhausted.

He needed air, openness.

Freshness.

Escape.

Solitude.

More than anything, he needed Potest Mountain. He needed to climb until his legs gave out, and his thoughts too. He would climb until he forgot it all that had happened, until he wasn't able to imagine what might happen in the future.

That's going to take a lot of climbing, he thought grimly but suddenly, he was up for the challenge, as long as it took him far away.

CHAPTER 4

Frankie

Was this really what I had in mind for some time away to think?

Frankie stared up at the failing light on her cracked plaster ceiling. Fifteen more minutes, give or take, and it'd be time...

Of course this wasn't what she'd had in mind.

She was a city girl, used to Richmond's long and varied list of things to do. There was a rotating schedule of concerts and festivals as well as the usual malls hang outs and parties. In the backwater that was Sagebrush, she'd envisioned long sunny afternoons meandering through gorgeous blueberry fields, letting the immaculate country air fill her head until everything became as clear as she needed it to be.

She reasoned that it was her own fault for relying on her childhood memories.

Growing up, weekends in the country at Uncle Elmer's had meant gobbling wild blueberries by the bucket and helping jolly Aunt Frida bake double cinnamon apple pies. It brought up memories of riding Juniper, the silly, spotted, brown pony who whinnied at every horse fly who dared enter her realm.

So much was different now and Frankie couldn't be sure if it was because of her flawed memory or because life had hardened her. Things had changed it seemed and not just the obvious. The wild blueberries hadn't survived the record-breaking frigid winter, Aunt Frida had died of pneumonia two years back, and Juniper had been moved to a farm in the next town where aging ponies were well cared for.

Frankie had been in Sagebrush for a week and her mind was anything but clear. She thought of how she'd come to be there, flopped on the hard-as-concrete, musky-smelling mattress and wondering what Uncle Elmer would do if she just disappeared. Maybe she could go stay at the farm where Juniper was. Surely she'd find some nice people to talk to over there. At least that would give her some reprieve from Elmer's unyielding foul mood.

Frankie knew it was a pipe dream anyway. She couldn't just off and walk to another county. Sagebrush wasn't exactly neighboring any other town. The nearest, Barleywood, was twenty-five miles away.

Buses didn't run there and her parents had traveled to France for the summer. Adelaide had stayed in Richmond to pursue some undisclosed academic pursuit. Frankie considered going back home but then she'd have to deal with her sister's equally annoying disposition.

Addy should have come here and hung out with Elmer. Those two would have been fast friends in their personalities.

It was still an option but Frankie considered it a last resort. She knew her sister wouldn't be impressed if she returned unexpectedly. Frankie had promised to stay on the farm, after all, even if it was proving to be a wasted journey.

In short, she was left to enjoy the few pleasures that Sagebrush had to offer for the next two months—if she could find them

So much for finding myself this summer.

Not that Frankie had exactly had high hopes when she'd paid lip-service to the universal right of exploring her options after high school. The idea of a gap year had sounded appealing and had all the allure a nineteen-year-old could want but she also knew that she couldn't find herself in a place like Sagebrush. Sequestering herself in some place where no one knew her and the closest Walmart was a two hour-drive away was hardly the Zen retreat she needed. When she really thought about what she was doing there, she realized the cold, hard truth of it.

I have no clue what I want to do with my life, and coming here for a while beats slogging off to some college I don't want to attend. It's probably better to be here than looking at all the same faces I've seen for the past nineteen years.

To be fair, Frankie loved her lively friends and the city but she couldn't ignore the tugging sensation that had started years ago. It had taken Frankie some time to understand it but when she did, it was like a slap to the face.

It's all getting really old and stale.

It was the same parties with the same people talking about the same things ad infinitum.

"What do you think college will be like?"

"Did you hear about the stuff that happened up in town?"

"Oh my God, did you hear that Ryan and Lucy are back together—again?!"

Inevitably, the same thought would cross through Frankie's mind as she zoned out their insipid conversation.

Is this all there is? Surely there's more to life...

She was full of internal scolding and flashes of annoyance that she couldn't get past all that she had going for her. But still, there it was.

She wanted more. She just wasn't sure how to get it.

Frankie stood up. It was dark outside, and she was tired of sitting around, feeling sorry for herself.

It was time to get the save-a-cat show on the road.

On her feet, Frankie grimaced at the wooden creaky floor while considering her options. Leaving the house without it creaking like an alarm would be no small feat.

Every footfall Frankie made in her knitted socks had to be carefully considered, delegated with the precision of an army sergeant. In return, the house provided only the softest groans, reserved for appliances or for no discernable reason. The house was old and temperamental, not unlike her Uncle Elmer.

At the bottom of the steps, Frankie paused. She tilted her head with her ear up, although there was no need. There it was, circling down from the attic. The loud, certain and oddly calming sound of Uncle Elmer's snorty snores.

Frankie caught her giggle with her hand just in time to stop it from ringing out into the house.

At least some things hadn't changed.

Uncle Elmer had the odd habit of sleeping like a dead buffalo and waking at the smallest provocation like an angsty hare. It was anyone's guess what might rouse him.

It took her a few seconds for her eyes to get used to the dark. Feeling her way along, she sighed remembering her request to add some outdoor lighting. Uncle Elmer didn't believe in "any extra money-filching outdoor lighting" (as he'd so flatteringly referred to her idea to add an outside lamp).

"When you get to bed at a civilized hour there's no need for frivolous things like that," he'd intoned. Frankie shook her head at the memory of the pleasure in his exaggerated tone when he'd pushed her suggestion aside.

She realized in that moment that his early to bed habit was her boon.

Goosebumps prickled Frankie's arms, despite the hoodie she was wearing. The air was chilly, and she was glad she'd thought to grab her jacket before leaving her room. She pulled it on now as she headed out to find the cat.

When she was several yards away from the barn, the chickens started clucking knowingly. Daphne snorted in her disapproving way, her porcine face coming into view. Frankie waited a moment, sensing his nearness and finally, the king himself materialized.

Raoul strutted through the missing barn door slab with his plumed belly at a puff indicating that mere doors were no match for him. He sashayed in front of Frankie and planted himself to block her entry with a beady look that she didn't misinterpret in the least.

"Don't you dare," she told him flatly. He opened his beak, and she took off around him and slipped into the barn, not swayed by his effort to keep her at bay.

Once she was inside, the animals were too quiet before full chaos ensued. A raucous slew of beastly noises filled her ears, each one outdoing the next. It was impossible to tell who was being louder as the chickens, pigs, and cows tried to outdo one another.

"Shush!" Frankie hissed, crouching and squinting through the darkness furiously.

She knew that using her phone's flashlight would be faster, but she worried that the brightness might irritate the animals more. She counted herself lucky that Raoul hadn't cawed. That was certain to wake Uncle Elmer.

"Gus?" she whispered tentatively in the new silence when the animals finally realized that she bore them no danger.

There was no response to her quiet call.

"Gus?" she tried again.

Still nothing except the noises of the barn animals she was hoping would soon settle down as they tried to reclaim their comfortable positions.

Suddenly, she was worried for the little cat. How could she have just left Gus alone here for that long? She had set him up in a blanket and fed him before Uncle Elmer had finally caught her but it had been a long while since she'd last seen him. Frankie was worried he might have gotten into it with one of the other animals.

Or fallen prey to a predator.

When she'd found him two days earlier, he'd been a pile of matted fur and bones, shaking so much he could barely open an eye. After she'd fed him a steady diet of hotdogs and water, he'd been a bit less shaky and woozy, but had been far from a picture of perfect health. He needed attention and she had left him.

"Gus?" she whispered, more forcefully this time.

A weak, displeased sounding meow and, close by, two yellowy orbs regarded her with imperious disinterest. As gently as she could, she leaned forward and swept the sickly kitten into her arms.

If he'd been stronger, Gus likely would have howled, hissed, and given her hand a good chomp before galloping off into the sunset. As it stood, he grew as stiff as a board in her arms, and a low whine rolled out of him. He was far too weak to protest her nearness.

"I know." Frankie kept her voice down as she exited the barn, sidestepped Raoul and continued on. "But we have to go fast or my uncle will catch us and freak, okay? That won't be good, so we'll have to be sneaky."

Whether he actually understood her or was just too tired to make any other noise, Gus seemed to relax in her arms slightly.

She walked as quickly as she could to get to safety with

her new friend. Frankie's Doc Marten jammed on a stone, and she stumbled and slowed down. She had a feeling she was already near the end of Uncle Elmer's property. She could just make out what was likely the broken-down fence line. Using one hand to brace herself, Frankie hopped over.

Ugh.

Frankie's whole body jerked back so hard she almost dropped Gus, the weak fence falling back with her. She was being pulled back and her heart leapt into her throat.

"I'm sorry!" she cried, as the kitten scrambled and dug his claws into her tie-dye hoodie to keep from falling to the ground.

And the award for worst cat rescuer goes to...

She held him to her tighter, while she craned her head around, expecting the worst—Uncle Elmer with a hand clamped down on her hood, his face reproving.

Yet when her eyes adjusted, she realized that it was only her mini-backpack strap, snagged on a part of the fence. She exhaled with relief.

"Home free," she whispered as she pulled her backpack to her side. She gave Gus a light scratch on his little head between his ears. "Dinner time."

She gently placed the cat on the ground. Crouching down, she grabbed the Ziploc of bacon out of her backpack. She was proud of how she'd snagged the extra rations hours ago while Uncle Elmer was in the bathroom doing his five-minute hand-scrubbing routine.

Gus was busy sniffing at the fence, but as soon as she opened the bacon bag, his head whipped her way. He trotted back toward her flopping onto his belly when he got there.

"There you go," Frankie cooed, stroking him as she held out a bacon piece. It was small, about the size of her fingernail, but still it took the poor kitten a good minute of furious gnawing before he could finally gulp it down. "You must have been starving. I'm so sorry I took so long."

The cat continued to shake, all skin and bones, but his swollen eye was beginning to open, if only slightly. Frankie tested the ground with her thumb. The mud and grass were cool, probably too cold for such a weak kitten. Best thing would be to scoop him up and tuck him into her sweatshirt while she fed him.

He was so light, even for his tiny size. Frankie felt like she was holding a small pile of feathers.

Once he was tucked into her jacket, propped against her chest, he tilted his head in an odd angle, causing Frankie to stare where he was looking. She wondered if it was the smell of the air or the sounds almost imperceivable to human ears.

A dog yowling at the moon in the distance.

Footsteps.

Hold on. Footsteps?

Frankie clutched Gus to her chest tightly at as the realization struck her full force. There was someone out there, headed her way.

CHAPTER 5

Logan

Dark blue velvet was the night sky. It reminded Logan of a dress he'd seen on an actress in a movie once. He'd been fascinated because it was the kind of material he could just tell was impossibly soft to the touch, even though he knew he'd never be able to touch it himself.

He didn't know how long he'd been walking for a long while—too long, probably. Yet he still wasn't sure he wanted to go back home, even though that was where he was headed. He passed the goat pen.

"Maaaa, maaaaa."

Logan stopped, a smile tugging at his lower lip. It was impossible to resist the goats and their ridiculous antics.

"Oh, all right Forti," he grumbled knowing that the beast was demanding attention. Forti gave out another victorious cry out as he neared.

Potens and Fortem were fast asleep in the corner of the pen but as always, Forti was raring to go. Logan gave the goat a good pat, noting that the hay and water bins were still well-stocked. The investment had turned out all right, for all Pa's grumblings. He hadn't wanted to keep goats. Even with Ma's suggestion of selling the milk and cheese for a profit, he'd never bought in to the idea. In the end, the goats came anyway. The twins had named the bulls—Ty Murray, Slim Pickens, James Sharp, for their favorite rodeo riders. Pa had named the wild horse Joan, and the chickens had been Ma's territory. Garrett had no opinion on animal names which left the goats for Logan to christen.

That first day, when the others laughed away at the comical beasts, Logan had seen the animals in a different way entirely. He observed how nobly they stood in the middle of the pen. They didn't run away and hide, even when they trembled with fear at their new surroundings.

For their troubles, Logan gave them noble names to match their noble bearings; Forti,(Latin for mighty), Potens (powerful) and Fortem (brave). Even though his brothers, especially the twins, mocked and taunted the goats, seeing the animals respond to their names gave Logan a silly twinge of pride.

He gave Forti a final scratch behind his ears and headed back toward the house. Logan tried to shake off the uneasiness that wouldn't go away. He felt like his world was out of whack but it had been that way since his father had died. He knew nothing would ever be right again.

His pace quickened as he moved, hoping that the change of scenery would do him good.

"Don't you worry, Ma, he'll be back before you leave. I know Logan, he wouldn't miss you leaving for anything."

Turning the corner toward the house, Logan stopped as though was he was hearing something he wasn't supposed to hear. A window on the ground floor was open and the voice belonged to Garrett. As for the prospect of facing him or Ma,

Logan turned on his heel and headed away from the ranch. It was dark out and high time he went on home, but he'd changed his mind. He wanted a bit more time outside with the fresh air, alone with his own thoughts.

He allowed himself to just wander the Thatcher property, toward the property line in a different direction than he usually went. The other area was more scenic, with the field flowers and the vegetable garden, and the big old willow tree. Yet another path threaded through their neighbors' properties until it eventually ended up at the Potest mountain range. But that night, he felt like going where he usually didn't, pushing his limits, seeing where he ended up.

Around this way, when he was young, a few of the neighbor's boys had jumped him. They'd gotten a few punches in before Logan could free himself but the memory overcame him in a tidal wave—because he thought those children were there in that moment.

The figure was still far off, near one of the dividing fences, but he could see someone sitting there with his denim-clad legs splayed outward, ready to rip out of the past and throttle Logan then and there.

Logan forced himself onward even faster. He knew he was imagining things, that it was a trick of the light.

I'm tired. I really should head home.

There was no one there, nothing to be afraid of. Just like the ridiculous situation with Ma, he was worried about nothing.

What would it be like to not be afraid for once in my life?

He found himself thinking about his father and how he hadn't said anything then either.

Logan stopped in his tracks, his thoughts evaporating until only one was left in place.

Whoa.

Seeing *her* was a spike of clarity straight into his veins, a combination of hot and cold overcoming him as his gaze drank her in.

Her hair the same intensity as red swirls of the wild strawberry jam he put on his toast every morning, eyes so blue, they must have taken the sky's pigment for themselves.

Lips curled into a sly, beam as if she knew something that Logan didn't and oh, how he wanted to know.

She sat with her legs swinging haphazardly, leaning forward just enough to make him question what she was doing there—was she about to say hello or spring to her feet and walk away without a word?

Seeing her brought him back to a place he'd never been.

Yet there they were...

Suddenly, he was back on the mountain, climbing. The hyper-realness of it all made him wonder if he was dreaming.

This girl in front of him wasn't real, couldn't possibly be. Logan knew everyone for twenty miles and this red-headed apparition was not from around there.

The way she was looking at him like *he* was the ghost. Her, with her clothes out of some 1960s movie—tie-dyed hoodie and high-waist jeans with retro buttons. That hair, eyes and face with the colors turned up to an almost painfully brightness. She was too vital, too alive in the quiet stillness.

She's definitely not a ghost.

She spoke.

"I don't have any money but I have a knife."

Her voice was laced with it too, that same intrinsic vibrancy, even amidst the threat and Logan felt himself flushing.

"Oh..." he muttered, realizing that he was threatening to her. "Sorry..."

Logan took a step back, then another to show her that he meant her no harm.

"I... um..." He faltered, trying to find the words he was looking for. "What are you doing here?"

"Me?" Her eyes narrowed as she got off the fence. It was then he realized she had the saddest looking cat he'd ever seen pressed protectively to her. "I'm not the one who's night-wandering and creeping up on people."

Her defensiveness startled him slightly and through the darkness, he continued to study her face, realizing that there was nothing country about this girl.

"I'm not creeping on people. Just wandering. I live here." He jabbed his thumb over his shoulder to indicate the ranch, feeling like a suspect telling a cop his alibi. "Sorry."

Why do I keep apologizing? She startled me just as much as I did her.

Yet he couldn't bring himself to feel upset by this woman in the least. He couldn't look away either.

She straightened, tugged on her hoodie drawstring, twining it back and forth like a pendulum. She eyed him warily and exhaled as she decided whether to believe him or not. Finally, she nodded.

"It's okay. I didn't mean to sound so jumpy. I just didn't expect to run into anybody out here. I mean sometimes you don't know who might be around."

"Makes sense. Though we don't really get too much trouble around here. Serial killers, I mean. They'd have to walk for ages, wait even longer and hope that we aren't carrying a hoe, shovel or that we aren't one of those trigger-happy farmers on TV."

She chuckled and it was musical. The cat at her chest stirred and mewled weakly. Logan's brow furrowed, realizing that the animal was in bad shape.

Logan peered at the cat.

"Is he okay?"

All the mirth fell away from her face as she, too, turned her eyes on the animal.

"Not really, no. I mean, he was like this when I found him, so he might be a bit better with the food and water I gave him but…"

"You found him around here?" he asked but his query was loaded.

Who are you and what are you doing out here?

Unfortunately, she only answered with a single word.

"Yeah."

They stood, looking at each other for a few seconds, an awkward silence falling between them.

Logan waited, hoping she would break the quiet between them but she didn't seem to have anything else to add.

"Well," he sighed, turning away to leave her in peace. "Be careful out here."

"I'm Frankie."

He pivoted back, catching the smile on her face and he relaxed.

"Logan," he offered, extending a hand toward her. She eyed it and laughed again, accepting the formal gesture. When they touched, Logan's heart picked up slightly as he felt the velvet softness of her hand. He cleared his throat, reluctantly releasing her hand.

"Listen, about tonight… I don't normally…" he started, feeling the need to explain more to her.

"Wander in the middle of the night and scare young girls?" Frankie offered.

She said it like it was a joke and Logan smiled.

"Nah, I save the scaring for the goats instead, get 'em to faint if I'm lucky."

She giggled and Logan grinned again at the sound. He was sure he would never get tired of listening to that on a loop.

"Clearly you've never scared a goat to faint before," he teased.

"It's that glorious, is it?"

Glorious.

He'd heard that word before, but never like that – with the strong 'r' that brought forth its full potential. Hearing Frankie use it made him want to use it more.

She was looking at him.

Ah. It's my turn to talk.

"Yeah, it is."

She gave her head a shake, and for a few *glorious* seconds all Logan could see was red waves undulating and filling his field of vision, then she transferred the hand to her hip. "Anyway, I'm not a girl."

"No?" He cocked his head to the side in question. Frankie howled with laughter, misunderstanding his inquisitive look.

"I just meant I'm not as young as I look."

Logan blinked at her.

"I'm nineteen," she continued. She waited a beat before her blue eyes swung his way. "You?"

"Twenty. Guess that makes me a man too, then."

Even if I don't feel like it most days.

Her smile was contagious.

"Guess it does," she agreed, a slight purr to her voice and Logan had a difficult time knowing where to look. His gaze darted from her eyes to her mouth and back up again. Her smile held a question, a promise and an inevitable disappointment.

Logan ripped his eyes away. He felt a strange combination of clear-headed, light-headed.

"So you live here with your family then, then?" she asked, forcing him back into focus before he could be carried off by the heady feeling.

"Yeah." Logan nodded as he rhymed them off. "With my brothers and Ma. My Pa—"

He abruptly stopped talking, wishing he could back up the night three minutes and start all over.

But Frankie was still there, still looking at him, waiting.

"Your father?" she asked.

Why not tell her?

"He died a few months back."

Her eyes widened a fraction.

"Oh, I'm so sorry."

"Thanks."

He didn't say anything to try to ease the moment because there was nothing to say, not without dredging it all up again and reopening old wound.

Frankie was still looking at him, like there was more to see. Logan shifted his weight onto his other foot.

"It was nice meeting you." The words were out before he could stop them. "I should be going. You have a good night now."

He turned before he could see her eyes change, before he could see her whole face telegraph what she thought of him.

Walking away, he knew full well that he had no reason under the moon to be leaving, other than the real one. The truth was, he wanted to leave before she decided to, before the spaces in the conversation started to annoy her, before his silence started unnerving her. He needed to get away before she could see him for who he really was.

So what if I never found out her full name and how she got here? It's too late now. Except...

He'd never found out if she was even okay, or lost. He could have helped her if she'd needed it. Should have helped her.

Logan paused, knowing full well already that Frankie was more than capable of taking care of herself.

I don't know if it's really safe for a young woman out there at night, do I? She's clearly not from around here...

"Wait!" he called, turning around at the same time.

She cocked her head at him and he saw that she hadn't moved a step in any direction from where he'd left her.

He strode over quickly.

"You need anyone to walk you home or someplace? These parts are pretty safe, but still, it's nighttime and I'm happy to help you out."

"I can take care of myself, thanks," she said coolly. Her entire disposition had changed and Logan knew he had no one to blame but himself for that.

Her closed lips and low-lidded eyes indicated that she'd made her mind up about him.

I'm not worth her time.

"Right," Logan muttered.

Leave it, Logey, you messed up again.

But he couldn't get his feet to budge. He felt like he was stuck in place, like something was forbidding him from walking away again.

It's cold tonight. Why am I sweating?

"Thanks though," she said, a little less standoffishly when she saw he wasn't moving away.

"Yeah, I..." Words continued to spill from his lips, beyond control of his brain. "How would you feel about going climbing with me sometime?"

The night got strangely quiet, the wind faltering in the wake of his words. He waited impatiently to see how she'd react, his body half-turned to sprint away as she stared at him.

You invited a strange, city girl climbing? Are you out of your mind? If she didn't shut you down before, she's going to now for sure!

"Okay."

Logan froze. He glanced back at her tentatively. But she didn't look like she was laughing at him. Her shiny raspberry combat boots planted in the dirt, chin jut out, she looked like she was testing him.

"Really?" he asked, dumbfounded by the response.

"Now?" she asked lightly.

"It's my favorite time…" He wasn't lying. Night-climbing forced him to focus completely and dig in to just how alone he was. In those times it was just him and the rock.

He couldn't actually ask her now now, not with the hurt cat and having just met her.

"Not now," he replied, grinning. "Tomorrow afternoon?"

"Okay."

"This is probably weird, I…" *Just want to see you again, somehow, somewhere, anywhere? No!* "…just thought it might be fun. Feel free to bring a friend or something. Although climbing isn't for everyone, so if you don't feel comfortable with it I understand."

First I couldn't talk at all. Now I'm rambling.

"I've climbed before. I'm up for it," Frankie replied and Logan's brow raised. He was impressed to hear that. She was smiling again, but it was a different beam. Logan wanted to know every one of her expressions and what they meant.

"Okay, so we'll meet here, tomorrow," he concluded. "Five good for you?"

"Five o'clock sounds good to me," Frankie agreed.

There was something in her stare, insolent and daring that made him want to catch her hand in his, say something, anything more in order to stay.

But now she was the one walking away, throwing up a hand.

"Night."

"Wait! You're sure you can walk you home?" he asked, suddenly emboldened now that she had agreed to a date.

She laughed and shook her head without turning around. "Night, Logan."

There was nothing left for him to do but wander back home.

The return to the ranch was silent, Logan enveloped in his own head. It wasn't the haze, but he wasn't bristling anxiety either. It was like after a good, long, hard climb.

His mind was clear.

Only later, when in his room back at the ranch did Logan realize that he still couldn't quite believe that Frankie was anything other than a night mirage.

Maybe she's not. Maybe I'm just crazy.

Yet the thought didn't stop him from falling asleep with a smile on his face.

CHAPTER 6

Logan

One bag? That's it?

Logan wouldn't have believed it if they'd told him. After all, his mind was cloudy from lack of sleep. Despite having gotten in early enough, he'd been unable to fall asleep until 4 a.m., an image of Frankie dancing in his mind until he finally succumbed to exhaustion. He half thought that was the reason his mind was playing tricks on him.

But there it was, in front of their oak front doors.

Ma and her *one* bag.

The woman who had packed for their rare family vacations as if they were moving houses. There had been extra pairs of everything for all four of them and Pa, "just in case." Pa would growl about having to make room for the bursting suitcases and tote bags but Ma didn't care. She brought everything along.

This time, though, for this trip of a lifetime, she'd packed one bag. She'd splurged for once and bought a new piece of luggage but it was only a small roller with a pull up handle. She looked wispy and small standing beside it.

In the past few months, she'd managed to lose more weight. Although right now, all geared up with a sure smile that seemed to hold up the rest of her face, she didn't look as fragile as she did before. She seemed effervescent.

Chance lifted his mother's bag and gave it a shake.

"Who are you, and what did you do with our mother?"

The boys laughed in unison.

"I packed her in there." Ma poked at an empty looking side pocket. "Didn't take up much room."

"Come on now," Garrett protested, but Ma held up a finger.

"Just kidding. Now please, let me thank you all again for this."

She closed her eyes, still smiling.

"For the longest time I just figured it was some silly dream. I was so sure that I couldn't do it. Even after your father... even after he... well, I just thought I was too old. I told myself that my life is here with you boys."

She waved a hand, tears springing to her eyes as they opened again. Chase squeezed her hand.

"Ma, we know. It's okay. We're going to miss you like crazy, but you have to do this."

"Besides." Chance bopped at the tickets sticking out of Ma's purple and white windbreaker pocket. "The tickets are bought. And, I mean, I *would* go, but there's the Houston Livestock Show and Rodeo and I'm in line to *win*, so I have to stay here."

Ma chuckled, while Garrett snorted.

"Regular martyr, you are."

A car horn sounded from outside. The dappled-glass windows beside the door showed a familiar sliver. The pea green with yellow and pink stick-on flowers of Mary-Ellen's Honda, waiting for Ma to come out.

"Ha," Ma said, though she suddenly didn't seem amused in the least. "That's my cue. Better get on with it."

They went to embrace her and it occurred to Logan, that he still hadn't said anything to his mother. He'd been lingering at the edge like a ghost until being pulled into the embrace of his family. Somehow, in the mix of all the arms, Logan's his head ended up closest to Ma's.

"You okay?" Ma asked, her voice close to his ear.

"I'm okay," he said, wishing his words didn't sound so hoarse.

The group fell back and Ma opened the door. A hot blast of morning air rushed in and another car horn blast split the silence. Mary-Ellen waved furiously from the open window grinning from ear to ear.

"You take care of her, you hear?" Garrett called out to Mary-Ellen as Ma got in the passenger's side.

Mary-Ellen winked.

"Can't make any promises. If she has too much fun…"

Ma stuck her head out the other side window, beaming.

"Bye, now!"

The car pulled away. It was happening fast, so fast, like someone was skipping sections in an online video. They were there and then they weren't.

"Bye!" he and the others chorused, racing out to wave as the car pulled out and down the driveway, turning onto the dirt road that eventually led to the highway.

Only Logan stood there until the car was a speck on the horizon. When he turned back to the house, the others had already retreated inside.

"Logan?" Garrett called, forcing him to retreat into the house and join the others. They sat in the kitchen, chatting and eating the mini apple cinnamon muffins Ma freshly baked before leaving. Logan popped a couple in his mouth to fill the emptiness inside him.

Things felt eerily normal.

It hadn't hit him completely that Ma was gone but he suspected it might later. He wondered if thoughts of Frankie were distracting him from feeling his mother's departure.

I have a date this afternoon, he thought, a grin creeping onto his mouth.

He forced himself not to think of Frankie as his date.

It's just climbing and who knows if she'll show?

"What you smiling about, Logey?" Chance asked. Instantly, the beam dropped from his face and he turned his head.

"Nothing," Logan muttered.

Frankie, Logan thought.

CHAPTER 7

Frankie

He isn't coming, is he?

Frankie folded her arms across her chest, a spike of anger shooting through her as she thought of how much she'd done to get there on time.

She'd sneaked out to feed Gus, loading her back tote with an obscene amount of some recently roasted almonds. She'd hurried through the few chores Uncle Elmer had time to grumble at her about while she was busy dodging him.

And it appeared to have been a wasted effort.

How dumb was she?

He was trying to get away and you didn't let him go.

But how he'd looked at her…

It wasn't easy to forget the way his eyes had drunk her in. Frankie was sure she'd never been looked at that way by anyone, least of all a stranger.

She tried to forget the pull she'd felt to him. She reminded herself that it had to be physical and understandably so. He was a fine specimen. Muscular and fit, handsome face in an imperfect way, tousled dark hair.

They sure do make them handsome down in the country.

Frankie refolded her arms and lifted her phone. Tapping the screen the time showed immediately.

4:59

She blushed at her overreaction. It wasn't even five o'clock yet. Not exactly high time for worrying with a minute to go.

What had gotten into her anyway? She was always late, if she even made it at all.

"Francis, what did we say about respect and timeliness?"

The voice piped through her subconscious as if it someone was yipping directly in her ear. Frankie dismissed the thought with a one-shouldered shrug and dug the toe of her Doc Marten into the dirt deeper and deeper.

I don't mean to be late all the time. Anyway, look what happens the one time I come early—

"Hey."

Frankie had been so mired in her own thoughts that she hadn't even heard him approach. The sound of his voice made her jump slightly but she quickly regained her composure.

"Hey," she replied nonchalantly.

She looked up and drank him in with clarity for the first time. The sunlight proved him to be even more gorgeous than she remembered.

"So we're really doing this?" Frankie teased.

"Was there ever any doubt?"

The deep green eyes set against his tanned complexion, seemed to belong to someone else. There was a pit of melancholy in them, one that faded slightly when he rested his gaze on her.

She quirked a semi-smile, willing away the sadness in his eyes.

"You tell me."

He smiled, shook his head.

"There wasn't. At least not for me."

His gaze has moved on already, over Frankie's shoulder. She turned to look herself and saw a hazy high mound on the darkening skyline.

"That's it?" she questioned, already knowing the answer. She couldn't imagine that he was taking her anywhere else at that hour of the afternoon and there wasn't anywhere else in eye's view.

"That's it," Logan conceded. "This way."

Frankie followed after him, marveling at his surefootedness. It was clear he knew the terrain by rote. She was certain that he could have found his way anywhere in those parts, blindfolded and somehow, that made her feel safe, protected.

Five different things to say jumped from one boundary of her head to the other. There were pretty wildflowers to point out, an overkill barbed wire fence someone had erected on the edge of their property. She saw how the sun had decided to play a final hide and seek with the ominous grey tufts of cloud in the sky and thought about whether he'd brought food in the pack on his shoulder.

Yet she let the questions and statements die on her lips after realizing that Logan made no effort to talk either. She wanted to know why he was so quiet. The more time she spent with him, the less he seemed to have to say.

Not that Frankie was opposed to being the talker of the two. Still, she found herself appreciating the silence between them, even though there was so much to discuss.

But after several long, heavy moments, she became uncomfortable with the quiet.

Frankie shoved her hands into her sweatshirt pouch,

wondering if she'd made a mistake agreeing to go climbing with Logan. The whole excursion was weird.

Who goes climbing with a complete stranger? Who is this guy anyway?

She wracked her brain for the remaining dregs of a sermon that Uncle Elmer had subjected her to on her first day in Sagebrush. Odd bits and pieces were coming back to her, but not enough to find answers to the burning questions she had at that moment.

In her mind's ear, she could hear her uncle prattling on.

"...And Mary-Ellen, she's an odd duck, oh yessir. Husband died, few years back, and since then, she's done things he'd never approve of... And don't you go going there, I'll warn you once and that's it... They're fine farming folk... Mean, real mean... Ain't much to be known 'bout those folks... Best rhubarb pie in the country... Thatcher boys..."

"You're one of the Thatcher boys, aren't you?"

Logan slung a look at her over his shoulder but he didn't seem all that surprised.

"Yeah. How did you figure that out?"

"Heard it."

"Okay."

"Yeah."

"So?"

"So what?"

A combination of frustration and annoyance shot through her.

"So what's it like, being a Thatcher boy?" she asked lamely, wishing she could think of something cleverer to ask.

His gaze was on where they were headed.

He probably wishes we're already there.

"It's like... you've got a good Ma, some fine brothers," Logan replied with just as little panache. Frankie stared at him, wondering if he was deliberately being short with her but he continued to walk, his expression shielded from her view.

"All right," she mumbled, reclaiming her trail. Silence thickened between them and by the time they finally reached the base of the mountain, Frankie wasn't sure about the climb anymore.

The mountain was a thing of beauty. It was tall beige-green swirl of grasses and cacti. Logan wasn't making any escape attempt, but he wasn't saying much of anything either.

Frankie simply wasn't convinced that she could handle another few hours of stinted conversation and she wasn't sure that Logan wanted to be there either.

Frankie came to an abrupt stop.

"I don't know about this."

Logan didn't glance her way.

"Don't worry, you've got this," he said. Frankie was almost surprised by the pep talk but she nodded slowly, even though he wasn't looking.

"No, yeah, I can do the climb. That's not what I meant."

He stopped walking and turned to look at her, his face clouding with understanding.

"Ah, right. Sorry."

Again, she found herself slightly confused by his words.

"For what?"

He raked a hand through his hair.

"I... It's not you, trust me."

"I know it's not me," she said defensively.

He smiled slightly.

"Well, now that we've established that..."

Frankie was annoyed.

"I'm serious. I think I may just head home."

Logan's features slackened, as his face went blank. He stood looking at her, saying nothing. For a long moment, there was only a heavy silence between them. Logan didn't beg her to stay nor cockily tell her to leave. In fact, there was no expression on his face at all.

"Wow." Frankie gaped at him when the quiet had gone on too long. "That's it? Nothing?"

She'd expected at least some half-hearted attempt to get her to stay, one that she would've batted away.

This guy is unbelievable. He's not even offering to walk me back.

She spun around, with her head held high, dismissing the thought that maybe she was the one overreacting in the situation but before she could take two steps, Logan's voice called out.

"Wait."

Frankie kept on going even though she wanted to glance back at him, if only to have a snapshot of him in her mind for later. Logan jogged to keep up.

"Frankie…"

"You don't have to walk with me," she said haughtily, even though she was secretly pleased he had come after her.

"I meant what I said before."

Frankie slowed slightly and gave him a look through her peripheral vision.

"About what?" she demanded. Logan sighed and looked away.

"I'm not always great with… people."

Well that's not shocking.

Frankie kept on walking, he kept on jogging but they were both going much slower now.

"What I'm trying to say is, I'm not so popular around here, even with my own family. I don't want to go giving you the wrong impression."

Frankie tossed him a contemptuous glare.

THE COWBOY'S ONE AND ONLY

"What makes you think I give two hoots about what anyone else thinks, here or anywhere else?"

"I don't know." His face was alive now with emotion, the change was invigorating. "Just—I don't always know what to say, so I just say nothing. It's easier."

She stopped at the ludicrous statement and stared at him in disbelief.

"Why?" she demanded. He looked away at her sudden scrutiny and Frankie ground her teeth. "It's fine, really."

She picked up her pace again and headed toward her uncle's face.

"Frankie…" Logan groaned, again hurrying to keep pace.

"Thanks for explaining it to me, but I don't want you to feel like you have to follow through with this just because you invited me," Frankie told him firmly.

"I don't," he said and Frankie could hear the sincerity in his tone.

"Really, I don't," he repeated. "I was actually looking forward to this."

Frankie arched a brow, again slowing her feet.

"And now?"

He shook his head bitterly.

"And now I figure this has gone how most things do."

"Which is?"

"I ruined something else."

There was regret in his voice and again, his eyes were clouded with that bone-aching sadness that broke Frankie's eyes.

Aw heck…

"Is that your way of apologizing?" she asked, trying to keep her voice neutral.

"Is that your way of saying that you'd forgive me if I did?"

Frankie didn't know what she'd do. All she knew was that

the cold hard certainty of walking away that had coiled in her belly was loosening.

"Frankie, I'm sorry I gave up on this before it really started," Logan murmured, his voice barely above a whisper.

Frankie snorted, wondering if he really believed that they were in a relationship.

"This? This is nothing."

Logan looked at her in disbelief.

"I apologized, didn't I?"

She nodded.

"You did. Want a cookie?"

He exhaled hard.

"You're a real piece of work, you know that?"

It was hard for her to understand, but Frankie found the back-and-forth invigorating, fun, feigning nonchalance and absolute confidence. After he'd thrown her head for a loop, it felt good to throw him one.

He slung one last look at her before his gaze settled on the mountain before returning to her face. She could tell he was trying to figure out where he stood with her but to her surprise, he bluntly asked.

"Think I'm going to go back. If I'm fast I can catch the sunset. Will you come too?"

"All right." Frankie replied. The man had jogged a good five minutes to keep up with her. She was beginning to feel foolish for her part in the drama.

He smiled, his face relaxing as he heard her response.

"Are you always such a spitfire?"

Frankie smiled on back.

"Guess you'll just have to figure that one out on your own."

They got back to the mountain's edge quickly enough. It started out fairly easy, but Logan picked out the supplies to be sure. As her eyes took it all in, he asked, "You sure you've done this before?"

"Yes," Frankie said immediately. Then she took a deep breath. "I mean, no."

In a sense I have, she reasoned but she could tell that Logan was waiting for an explanation.

"I climbed onto the roofs of some buildings with friends back in Richmond at the odd party, then onto this huge tank that was outside of some war museum, but that's about it. I've never really climbed out in the wild."

Logan appeared amused by her characterization.

"Ah. You'll still do fine."

His easy expression jabbed at the cartwheels of anxiousness going on in Frankie's abdomen.

"You don't know that."

He met her challenging glare with a bland look of his own.

"I do, though. Because you've got me. I won't let you fall."

The words sent an unexpected spike of warmth through her but she covered the heady sensation with a smirk as he dressed her in climbing gear.

"You some kind of climbing national champion?" she teased.

"Not that, no. But I've been climbing for years now, mostly on the Potest mountain range, but I'd like to think I know my stuff."

"What is Potest for anyway?" she asked curiously.

Logan eyed her evenly.

"How do you know it means something?"

"Wild guess." Frankie shrugged. "My parents forced me to take a bunch of language courses, and the word sounds familiar."

"Good guess. It's the Latin word for impossible."

"Ah, okay." Frankie swallowed, finding herself speechless

for a change. Logan had another set of climbing gear in hand, some that was a light pinkish color, and then it was time for them to start.

"You often go climbing with other people?" she asked lightly.

"Nah, I—" He clamped his lips shut as before he could finish his thought.

"What?"

His mouth spread into an unwilling line.

"I just... express ordered them, late last night. The gear. I realized you probably didn't have any, and I just had the stuff for me."

Frankie couldn't help but smile.

"I can pay you for it," Frankie offered, feeling sheepish. "I had no idea–"

"No." His tone was gruff, final. "I wanted to."

They let that sit there for a moment, it settling like a warm blanket around Frankie.

He wanted to.

"It's not often I get the opportunity to climb with someone else," he said easily, holding up what looked to be a harness thing. "Anyway, you know how to put this on? Or should I help?"

"Unless it goes around my shoulders, then yeah, I don't have the foggiest."

Logan chuckled as he crouched down.

"Yeah, not exactly."

It was only as she felt it sliding up her legs that Frankie realized where it was headed. Her hand stopped his. "Think I can take it from here."

Logan was red-faced and quiet; he simply nodded. Frankie tightened the thigh straps, every inch of her buzzing with how close he'd been. He clipped on a rope, then advanced towards the rock wall.

THE COWBOY'S ONE AND ONLY

As Logan set up the top rope anchor and bolts, Frankie let her gaze wander up higher and higher until she was slightly dizzy.

"You good?" Logan asked.

Frankie could only nod. Although the start didn't look terrible, she was painfully aware that she was looking at one tall mountain.

We're really doing this!

Next second, Logan was by her side, almost touching her.

"Hey, you can do this, you know that?"

Frankie wished she shared an iota of Logan's conviction.

"I mean it. You, you're tough," he insisted.

Again her whole body vibrated with the rebellion, the certainty of her internal speak.

You don't know that, you don't know me. But one tentative glance at his face, still so very close, revealed the truth. Somehow *he did.*

Frankie swallowed back her fear, nodded.

"Let's do this."

And so they did, one rocky handhold and easy-to-find foothold at a time. It was easier than she thought, less scary. Before she knew it, the ground was a far fall away, and she was laughing at it. Logan looked back at her, grinning himself.

"Feels good, doesn't it?"

Frankie inhaled a big breath of air, danced her gaze around taking it all in. The purple mountain laurel, thumb-shaped rock formation, the super handsome man a bit ahead of her.

"Feels great, actually."

It registered around her collarbone and lips as a happy buzz. It was obvious that Logan was a different man when he was climbing. She'd seen a hint of it at the base of the mountain, but now it was full blown. When he was climbing, he was certain, confident, jokey and in control. His face was bright in a way Frankie had only seen that one time, the night that she'd met him.

She could see why. There was something about climbing that made sense, which was both freeing and controlling simultaneously. Frankie was sure she'd never been so exhilarated.

Still, she was grateful once Logan patted a roomy ledge they'd made it to, and declared it time for a break.

Logan eyed her oddly, sitting with the rocky cliff the back to his chair and she smiled when she met his gaze head on.

"What?" she asked. "Why are you looking at me that way?"

Logan's expression didn't falter, his eyes intently fixed on her face.

"I have something to show you," he said.

Is that a good thing or bad thing? Frankie wanted to know. She had a feeling she was about to find out.

CHAPTER 8

Logan

His eyes couldn't decide where to look. The beauty flaming out in the sky before him, or its reflection in the beauty seated beside him.

When he'd told Frankie that he had something to show her, she'd suddenly grown quiet and cautious, like she understood what precious fragment he was giving her. It was something he'd never shown to anyone ever before, something that had always just been his and the mountain's.

But now she was there beside him, their arms lightly touching, her head back, lips parted, experiencing it, observing the blazing colors lighting the sky.

There was no adrenaline buzz, no snappy back and forth. Just nature showing them a splinter of her perfection, the two of them, sitting on the elevated rock with aching arms and legs and spellbound minds.

Logan couldn't stop himself from looking over at Frankie. His mind couldn't accept what was happening, that he was up there with not only someone else but a woman as beautiful as Frankie.

"I can see why you come here," Frankie murmured, her voice husky with emotion. It was clear to him that he was feeling just as much of the magic as he was.

She really gets this.

He wondered if she might be able to get *him* too.

For a long while they sat, watching the rays slant away, the beauty crumble and reform into a different kind, not a word exchanged between them until finally, he fully turned to stare at her face.

"Where did you come from?" Logan asked reluctant to break the silence between them. Frankie looked baffled by the question.

"Oh. Didn't I say?" she chuckled. "Richmond, Virginia."

He had heard the southern drawl to her words but he hadn't been sure where in the south she was from.

"And what, pray tell, are you doing out here in Sagebrush?" he asked.

You were really sent from the heavens, weren't you?

He said none of that, knowing how cheesy it sounded, even in his own head but it didn't change the fact that he felt as if she had been sent there for him.

"I don't know yet," Frankie replied slowly.

"That's all you're going to tell me?" Logan teased.

She smiled, and it seemed to crack open her face.

"That's all I'm going to tell you." She gave a little laugh. "Wow, I feel... I feel different."

"I feel different too." He meant it. It wasn't just the mountain air. He'd always felt more alive and energized when climbing. It was something about being around Frankie. She changed the atmosphere, somehow charging it with her energy.

"Your brothers don't like you?" she asked, out of nowhere.

He frowned, feeling the tug back to reality. He half-wished she hadn't gone in for the jugular so swiftly.

"Did I say that?"

"Kinda."

Logan paused and thought about it.

Do my brothers like me?

"They're my brothers," he said simply. "They love me, I'm sure but…"

He trailed off and thought about it.

"I'm very different from them. And I guess I'm different than most others around here. People don't know how to be around someone like me."

Frankie eyed him speculatively but Logan thought he saw a glimmer of understanding in her eyes.

"I feel that way sometimes too."

When he glanced at her, her face looked like it was still deciding what to think.

"Something tells me you get along with most people just fine."

"That's not what I meant… Just, ah!" She breathed through her mouth in exasperation. "I don't know what I meant. Just trying to make conversation."

Logan wished he hadn't said anything.

"All right."

Logan leaned his head back onto the rock. Her baggy sweatshirt still didn't hide her lovely shape, all swells and dips where there should be. A dimple was quirked in her cheek, like she was thinking about smiling but hadn't committed. Another long silence passed between them.

"We should be going back," he murmured after a moment.

Frankie didn't respond and Logan didn't say it again, unsure what her quiet might mean. This was entirely new territory to him. Frankie was new territory to him.

"Can we just stay for a bit longer?"

He jerked his head up and nodded in agreement, relaxing slightly as he realized she was still enjoying herself.

Time and reality began to blur as conversation began to flow between them. The only breaks they took in their discussion was to take in the beauty of the cool night or snack on one of the almonds that Frankie brought.

They talked about high school and how they'd both hated it. He told her about farming and Frankie found it amazing Logan had grown up tending to animals and riding horses.

"Some of my best childhood memories are of my aunt and uncle's pony," Frankie sighed, her eyes taking on a faraway look.

"Not a lot of farms in the city, huh?" Logan asked dryly.

"Not where I'm from at least," Frankie conceded.

They also talked about their families and found out they'd had some similar experiences. Her parents were traveling and so was Logan's Ma. Frankie didn't see eye to eye with her sister on a lot of things, same for Logan with his brothers. In some ways, Logan felt like he'd found a kindred spirit in Frankie.

Finally, the conversation turned to the time, something they had both been subconsciously avoiding until the last possible moment.

"What time you think it is?" Frankie frowned, almost as if she instantly regretted asking the question.

"I don't know, eight maybe?" Logan guessed.

The answer was wishful thinking. They had been talking a really long time and he had a feeling it was later than that.

"I'm sure it's still early." Frankie's voice was hopeful as she fished her phone out of her pocket. Then, a sharp intake of breath.

"What, is it? Ten?" Logan asked, already preparing the excuse he'd use for his grumpy brothers.

Sorry, lost track of time, sorry, I'll help with the dishes tomorrow, promise.

"Not quite that early." Frankie's voice was hushed. "It's one. In the morning."

Logan sat bolt upright.

"It's *what?*"

Frankie shoved her phone in his face. There, in inescapably glowing letters that burned into his retinas, there it was.

1:02 AM.

He scrambled to his feet.

"Oh gosh, I'm sorry. I wasn't thinking, wasn't keeping track…"

"Neither was I," Frankie said in a small voice that got smaller as she peered the way they came. "Are we going to have to… I mean, is it safe?"

"Yes, night climbing's safe," Logan assured her. "But do you think it's better that we spend the night here?"

His heart leapt and then did a belly flop onto reality's cold, hard floor. That would get his brothers into a riot.

"No." Frankie got to her feet, shaking her head. "No, that's impossible. Better if we get this over with, get home as soon as we can, so people won't worry."

She sighed, the worry on her face almost palpable.

Logan couldn't disagree with that. Hurriedly yet carefully, he set up their climbing supplies and headlamps, then looked to Frankie.

"Right. Let's go then."

The whole way down his focus was trained to a crack. Frankie was skittish and tentative in the dark, rightly so. Even for himself, night climbing was more challenging, Logan could only imagine the strain it was on Frankie, too.

She was above him though, so if anything happened…

He wouldn't let anything happen.

Nothing will happen to her on my watch. I won't let it.

In the end, they made it down unscathed. He'd chosen an easier climb since he didn't know her skill level and he was suddenly grateful he'd sensed she wasn't experienced.

Soon, they were walking back, and Logan was struggling to make conversation. He asked her lame questions, like whether she missed Richmond or if climbing was how she expected it to be.

Finally, Frankie cut him off.

"It's okay now, we don't have to talk."

"What do you mean?"

In the dark, he couldn't make out her expression and he couldn't gauge how she was feeling. It was hard to miss the almost palpable tension radiating from her body but that had to be because of the time.

Didn't it?

He wondered if he was overthinking. Again.

"Just," she continued, as though choosing each word carefully, "After climbing with you and then seeing the beauty you showed me, I don't find the silence the same. Do you?"

"No." He realized it as he said it, let a silence stretch a little just to be sure. "No, I don't."

It was impossible, them having already attained the same comfortable silence people who'd been together for ages could enjoy. It was there, they were walking with it, all the way back to their respective properties.

Although it wasn't entirely comfortable for Logan, this was new ground for him.

There's a lot of new ground with her, isn't there?

This was only the first day. He wondered what what the upcoming days would bring.

His mind trailed to his homecoming after he saw Frankie back.

He'd annoyed his brothers in a number of inadvertent yet

unique ways. Once he had failed to cover for Chance when he'd snuck out to see some wild girlfriend. Another time, he'd wandered off and missed the family dinner he'd promised to help with.

But this was different. This wasn't Logan Thatcher getting lost in his own head. This was something more precious than that and he knew his brothers would demand an explanation, one that Logan didn't want to give.

It wasn't just that he didn't want to, he physically couldn't. Telling them or anyone else about Frankie was out of the question. He didn't want to let anyone else in on his secret. Certainly not yet and perhaps not ever.

There was something pure about what they had. Pure and simple—easy even.

All Logan knew was that he wanted to spend more time with Frankie, in any way he could. He didn't want his brothers tainting it, trying to shove it into a premature definition, making sly comments and hinting at things. He didn't want unsolicited advice or a slew of questions he wasn't even sure he could properly answer.

I'll slay that dragon when I come to it, he told himself firmly. For the moment, he was still in Frankie's spell and he didn't want to waste a minute souring it with outside thoughts.

"I'll walk you all the way home," he said once they paused at the fence where they'd met.

"I'll be fine," Frankie said quickly. "I got home just fine by myself last time, remember?"

"I'm not making the same mistake again," Logan said firmly.

Frankie sighed loudly.

"Oh, all right."

Through the corner of his eye, Logan could see her fighting a smile and it pleased him to know that he had pleased her.

As they neared the house, Logan realized just where they were. He paused in mid step.

"You live with Elmer Mills?"

"Yeah, he's my uncle. And he's probably waiting by the door with a knife, so it would probably be best if we say goodbye here."

Frankie bit her lower lip as she came to a stop, a few feet away from the bottom of the steps. Though the window shutters were closed, a thin light from within was visible in the dark.

"That's just what I need, him accusing me of being an irresponsible trollop, as well as an inconsiderate guest."

Logan didn't meet her joking yet nervous smile. He planted his feet firmly.

"I'm not going anywhere. You can go in, and I'll wait outside in case he... I don't know. In case you need help explaining."

Frankie chuckled.

"Uncle Elmer's bad temper is renowned around here too?"

Logan snickered.

"Aside from his blueberries, it's about all he's known for."

But Frankie's smile was dying fast.

"About today, the climbing, everything... thank you."

"Thank you for coming. And for forgiving my social ineptitude."

Frankie giggled, stabbing up a finger.

"You're not socially inept. You just don't give yourself a chance."

Logan just shrugged.

"Whatever it is, thanks."

She nodded, not moving.

"You too." She took a step away, then paused, as if there was something more. "See you around."

"Definitely." Logan bobbed his head. "Now that I know where to find you. Oh, and good luck."

"Thanks. I'll need it."

Frankie turned away from him, settled her shoulders, strode forward before darting up the steps. As she opened the door the porch light came on and Logan moved a little off to the side, ensuring he was out of Elmer's view as he watched the scene unfold. While he was happy to help if need be, he also didn't want to provoke a worse outburst from the man if it wasn't necessary. He hadn't been joking when he said that Elmer's foul moods were legendary in those parts and it didn't help that Elmer Mills had never liked Logan.

As soon as the door slammed with a bang, he knew there would be no provoking a worse outburst. It was starting out badly without his help. Logan didn't need to strain to hear the shrill berating tone of Elmer's voice.

"My, oh my. My own niece!" Elmer roared over Frankie's protests. "She comes to me, beggin' to stay, beggin' to get away from her terrible hard life! And then what does she do? Just what does she do?"

The next short stretch of silence was only for dramatic effect. His voice thundered over Frankie's attempted response.

"She disappears off the face of the Earth for hours! Half the night! Keeps me up worryin' and thinkin' she's dead in a ditch somewhere! Called everybody I know and nobody's seen her. She's just gone without a word! Not a bye-bye, just nothin'!"

"Uncle Elmer," Frankie tried reasonably as Logan watched helplessly from the shadows. "If you'd just let me explain I'll tell you everything."

"I ain't finished My own flesh and blood niece, gone! Then she turns up here in the middle of the night and—"

"There you are!" A new voice joined the fray and Logan couldn't help but strain now, curious as to who else was there.

"Adelaide?!" Frankie jerked her head around in shock. "Why are you here?"

"I told you I'd come down here myself if you didn't listen to sense, didn't I?" the newcomer said in a chiding tone.

"But–"

"I gave it a week, but when you still didn't come back, I knew what I had to do," Adelaide declared.

Uncle Elmer loaded this as new ammunition.

"Not even a word to your own sister! What was I to think? What was I to tell my only brother? That I'd lost his daughter? There's no telling what could have happened!"

"Is she okay?" Still another voice. This one made Logan's blood run cold. It made him want to run back to Thatcher Farm without looking back once.

Logan knew what he'd find there—an empty farmhouse. His brothers were at Elmer's.

Garrett stepped onto the porch and Logan ground his teeth, the euphoria of the night fully evaporating.

"Fine as fine can be. Though she won't be, I can promise you that," Elmer growled maliciously. Logan was beginning to wonder if Elmer was physically going to hurt Frankie. His back tensed, ready to spring at the thought.

"And our brother?" Chase asked, coming onto the porch with Chance.

Logan groaned, knowing that the gig was already up. He knew what he had to do, just as well as he knew it was the last thing in the world he wanted to. He stepped back to the bottom of the stairs and looked up.

"I'm here," he said, and six pairs of eyes snapped his way.

"What in the heck?" Chance demanded, storming out to

THE COWBOY'S ONE AND ONLY

meet him. "You couldn't send, I don't know, a text or something?"

"You!" Elmer shrieked, lurching his way, finger stabbing out. Garrett and Chance caught him by his arms just in time. "I swear if I find out that you've been—"

"It's not what you think!" Logan interrupted.

Elmer struggled against Garrett and Chance, still yelling as if he hadn't heard a word.

"You boys let go of me. I can't believe you dared to even talk to my niece! I always knew there was something off about you, boy, but this.. this takes the cake!"

Adelaide was trying to say something too, while Garrett and Chase struggled to talk Elmer down.

"Everyone just be quiet!" Frankie yelled, her voice overshadowing the ruckus.

Stunned, all eyes turned to her.

"There, isn't that better?" Frankie said sweetly. "Now, before you all go having a collective aneurysm, Logan and I were just climbing. That's all."

"*Climbing?*" Elmer said, mopping his brow with a suspicious expression like she had referenced a new type of designer drug.

Logan nodded.

"Climbing the Potest Mountain."

Elmer squinted at him like he was trying to gauge the veracity of his statement.

"But…but why?" he finally muttered.

"For fun," Logan replied.

The look on Elmer's face said he didn't believe a word of it.

"Our brother is way weird," Chance confirmed cheerfully. "But harmless, honestly."

"We didn't even hug goodbye when he walked over with

me a few minutes ago," Frankie chimed in, with a slightly disappointed expression that Logan filed away for later.

Although Uncle Elmer was far from appeased, he was shaking his head the way he did whenever anyone tried to bargain down his blueberry price.

"That's bunk. Ain't no one climbing at this ungodly hour. Can't see, for one thing."

"Obviously, we didn't set out just now," Frankie cut in. "It was light when we got there, we climbed a bit, then we saw the sunset, then…"

She realized at the same time Logan did, too late. This was where it would get dicey with how the others saw it.

"Then what?" Chase asked, his eyebrows pulled in an honestly curious expression.

"Then we just talked," Logan said, feeling like he was under a microscope.

Uncle Elmer snorted.

"Just talked? For hours?"

"Yes, we did," Frankie said, shoving both hands into her pockets. "I'm sorry we were late and made you worry, but we honestly just lost track of time, and hurried back as soon as we realized how late it was. And if you don't believe us, then that's your problem not ours, so there! Goodnight!"

She stormed off into the house, but stopped on the threshold and turned around to fix her eyes on his.

"Bye Logan!"

She disappeared into the house before he could respond but Adelaide chased her down.

"Hold on there, you're not getting off the hook that easy," the woman who Logan now knew was Frankie's sister cried. "Did you really not tell him?"

The screen door slammed in their wake but Logan's stomach lurched.

Tell me what?

From inside the house, Logan heard Frankie demand, "Tell him what?"

"Come on," Adelaide grumbled. "He has a right to know."

There was a long silence as everyone stared uncomfortably at one another, unsure if they should stay or go but suddenly, two red tinged heads reappeared on the porch.

"Why? I have to give every guy I go climbing with a full account of my history?" Frankie hissed in a low voice.

"Fine, if you won't tell him, I will," Adelaide said smugly, turning to look at Logan. "Frankie has a boyfriend."

Logan felt like a bucket of ice water had been dumped on his head but when he looked at Frankie, she shook her head vehemently.

"I do not," Frankie snapped. "I broke up with him."

"You didn't mean it," Adelaide said simply. "You just need some time to think."

Frankie groaned and threw her head back.

"I've had more than enough time to think. Why can't you all get it through your heads? I don't want to be with Andrew anymore."

"They were going out for a year." Adelaide addressed Logan again. "Just so you know. She promised she'd see him, after this."

"That was just to get him off my back!" Frankie protested. "And to make sure he'd let me come here without him tagging along breathing down my neck every second!"

Garrett raised a hand, putting an end to the Thatcher boys' role in the drama.

"All right, okay. Sounds like it's time for us to go. Thanks for calling us up Elmer."

Elmer aimed an evil eye at Logan.

"Better not have to do it again."

Chance took Logan by the arm.

"Come on, we've had enough excitement for one night."

Logan shrugged him off but casting Frankie a final look, he followed after his brothers, even though he wanted to stay and demand the entire truth from Frankie.

On the way back, Garrett tried talking to him a few times. "What were you thinking?"

Chance answered for him with a wink.

"That's our Logey for you… he wasn't."

Finally, Chase said diplomatically, "We're all tired. Why don't we try this on for size in the morning? Everything will be clearer in the light of day."

Chance made a dismissive sound.

"In the morning, I'll be on Slim Pickens, getting myself a nice practice in. But you boys can do what you want."

Logan didn't have an energy left to say anything. His head felt like it had swelled two sizes, then deflated, leaving an extra space of emptiness.

Inside the house, with the welcoming whoosh of apple cinnamon, he remembered.

Ma's gone too.

Only thing to do was to stagger to his bed, collapse onto it, and hope for sleep.

CHAPTER 9

Frankie

"Morning sunshine!"

Frankie rolled to her other side, balling her pillow firmly around her head, trying to block out the sing-song tone of her sister's voice.

"Go away."

"Come on," Adelaide protested. "You can't ignore me forever."

Frankie rolled on her back to glare at her sister, who was wearing a pink oversized tee shirt printed with smiling yellow rubber ducks. "Number one, oh, yes I can. Number two, it's been, like, five minutes already."

"Like ten." Adelaide was smiling their firm mother's smile. "And no, you can't. I'm your sister."

"You're a nuisance."

"I'm a help."

"A terror."

"A comrade."

"The bane of my existence."

Adelaide sighed loudly and ripped the pillow away.

"Seriously Frankie, you only have yourself to blame for this."

Frankie propped herself on her elbows so she could glare at her sister unencumbered.

"Oh. So it's *my* fault that *you* gave Logan the totally wrong impression about Andrew and me?"

Adelaide assumed the innocent expression the sisters had perfected.

"You *did* go out for a year, didn't you?"

"Yes, all right, a year!" Frankie grabbed the pillow back and hugged it to her. "One boring year of bland dinner dates and me wanting to break up with him until I finally did it. It wasn't exactly the romance of the century."

"You never gave him a chance," Adelaide insisted firmly.

"*You* never gave *me* a chance," Frankie shot back. "You never believed that maybe, just maybe, I knew myself and my own mind enough to know that after a year, this guy was boring with a capital B."

"Still." Adelaide had started to pace, her stress move. "He was better than those other guys, Jared and um… what was the smoker's name?"

"Mark. And he smoked cigars, like, once a week."

Adelaide gave Frankie a look like that settled it.

"You're supposed to be my sister," Frankie protested, "You're supposed to support my choices."

"Only when they're good ones," Adelaide chirped in her irritatingly chipper way.

"No, that's our parents' job."

Adelaide snorted.

"We both know what they're like."

"Yeah, I do." Frankie was suddenly, hopelessly sad, and hugging the incredibly thin pillow didn't help. "Which means that more than anything I need a sister who supports me."

If Adelaide caught the sad plea, she didn't show it.

"I'm your older sister. It's my job to protect you. If I see you doing something wrong, you're darned right I'm gonna say something."

"Whatever. In any case, it's definitely not your job to play matchmaker for me. Why don't you concentrate on finding a nice boy for yourself? Take Andrew, if you think he's so grand. Honestly."

Adelaide gasped at Frankie, her face paling.

"I could never."

"I legitimately wouldn't care. If you like him so much, then go for it."

Addy shook her head and looked away. Frankie sighed loudly.

"Listen, I get the normal concept that I should be attracted to Andrew," Frankie continued, knowing it was pointless. "On paper, he's perfect but I don't want to be with him. Okay? And pressuring me about it, just makes me feel worse."

Adelaide was silent, clearly seeing that she wasn't going to win this fight. Finally, she said, "How much do you even know about this Logan guy?"

Frankie eyed her sister warily, unsure if she was winning her argument or giving Addy more ammunition.

"Not much," Frankie admitted.

"His brothers were... nice." Adelaide rotated her pacing to the wall, but not fast enough that Frankie missed her cheeks reddening. Frankie's eyes popped open with the realization.

"Aw, you like one of them!"

"No..." Adelaide said in a half-hearted, totally unconvincing voice.

"Which one was it?" Finally, Frankie was having fun. She

wracked her mind for what Logan had told her about his brothers. "Is it one of the twins? Chase or…Chance?"

Addy's blush deepened.

"Garrett," Adelaide said quietly. "The blond one. He seems really nice."

Frankie couldn't remember her sister being interested in anyone as long as she'd known her. There was always some minor nothing that was off about the guys she went out with. She nitpicked which was why her first dates rarely led to second ones.

"When's the wedding?" Frankie quipped.

Adelaide spun around to glare at her.

"Never. I'm probably never going to see him again."

Frankie whistled low.

"Well, lucky for you, I plan to be seeing lots of Logan Thatcher, so I'll pass the message along."

"What message? I don't have a message for him."

"Yes, you do. The message is that you like him and want to go out with him."

Adelaide's lower jaw dropped, her eyes bulging with horror.

"Don't you dare!"

Frankie was on her feet too, holding her duvet as a cape around her bare shoulders. She was enjoying this thoroughly. "Or what? You'll sic Uncle Elmer on me?"

"I don't need to." Now it was Adelaide's eyes glinting with satisfaction. "Didn't you hear his proclamation last night?"

"Uh, no? I was asleep before I hit the bed." Frankie had run upstairs, thrown herself in bed and fallen fast into dreamland, despite Elmer's hollers.

"He said that you're grounded." Adelaide crossed her arms across her chest. "For a week."

As if Frankie couldn't work out the unfortunate implications of this for herself, Adelaide added, "Which means you're stuck with the two of us. And farm work, of course."

Frankie gaped at her, a laugh of disbelief escaping her lips.

"What does he think I am, nine? I'm a grown woman, he can't *ground* me!"

"You're just lucky he didn't kick you out," Adelaide said smugly. "I'd swallow my pride if I were you and take my grounding."

Frankie snorted.

"And lose his free labor to do all the farm chores for him? I don't think he's crazy enough to risk losing the help."

"I'm here now." There was an odd tilt to Adelaide's chin as she said it. "So there's that."

"Hold on." Frankie circled her sister. She didn't like the sound of that. Not one bit. "I thought you were just visiting. Visits have end dates."

"You're just visiting too," Adelaide pointed out airily. "The way I figure it, as long as you're here, I should be here too."

Frankie dropped her duvet cape to the floor with a groan. "No."

"Why not?" Adelaide genuinely looked hurt.

"This was *my* idea, *my* trip. My chance to get away, enjoy myself. How am I going to do that if you're here pooh-poohing every last thing I do? It's bad enough with the uncle, with you here too it will be unbearable."

"Staying out until two thirty in the morning climbing isn't–"

"I didn't mean to do that! And I won't do it again. Good grief! Are you really that hard up for summer plans that you have to steal mine?"

Adelaide was quiet, looking at her hands and shame overcame Frankie.

Back home, Adelaide hadn't had nearly the same amount

of friends Frankie had. She was quieter, more reserved and even a little prim. Her social calendar was anything but full.

It hadn't occurred to Frankie that maybe Adelaide hadn't just come here to bother and mother her.

She came because she's lonely at home by herself.

"Never mind, it's all good," Frankie said. She flopped back on her bed. "I just don't want you breathing down my neck every time I get a fun idea."

"I have my own things to do too, you know." Adelaide was halfway to the door, her stiff back had relaxed slightly when Frankie gave in. "And you should remember that just because something isn't allowed doesn't make it fun."

Frankie couldn't help but smile.

"Ah, but it really helps."

Adelaide sighed heavily.

"Anyway, I should get started on the tomato picking."

"Have fun, I'll see you later," Frankie called after her.

Adelaide waved to her with a dubious expression.

"We'll see about that."

Frankie kept her face semi-worried until her sister was out of the room. It was really too bad for them.

Frankie knew this game better than anyone.

If Uncle Elmer thinks he's keeping me cooped up for two weeks, he's got another thing coming.

CHAPTER 10

Logan

"Um, I think they're good?" Chase said, while passing by, his eyebrows raised with amusement.

Chance laughed aloud when he saw what Logan was doing.

"Dude, you've been stirring up the eggs for like an hour. What are you hoping they'll walk out of the bowl and magically turn into pancakes themselves? I think pancakes have more stuff in them than eggs…"

"Go away," Logan muttered, his cheeks growing warm.

He clenched the wooden spoon tighter. As annoying as it was, his brothers were right. He'd lost track of time and what he was doing. He'd been thinking about that other thing so much. He needed to get his head in the game.

Someone's stomach growled. With a tactful side glance Logan's way, Chase asked, "Will the pancakes be ready any time soon?"

"Yeah," Logan sighed.

He didn't plan on messing around anymore. He was already sick of his brothers' covert leers and overt innuendo about what had transpired the previous night.

"I'll get another ride on Slim then," Chance said, Chase following behind him.

Garrett entered the room as the twins departed. He lingered by Logan's right-hand side for a few seconds as Logan added the last few ingredients to the batter. Logan's whole body tingled with the intrusion.

"Yeah?"

"Um, your friend, Frankie…"

Logan's jaw tensed.

"What about her?" Logan growled, expecting to be barraged by questions but when his brother spoke, he was slightly taken aback.

"Did…did she mention anything about her sister?"

Logan shot his brother a curious, wide-eyed look. The question took him aback slightly.

"Not really," he replied slowly. "Just that they didn't see eye to eye on a few things."

Garrett chuckled and stepped back, giving Logan some more reign of his personal space.

"Yeah, I gathered that much. Just… what did she seem like to you?"

Logan put down his spoon.

"Huh?"

"Just your impression of her." Garrett waved his hand at the bowl. "You don't have to stop what you're doing or anything, it's not important."

"Yeah, didn't really have a chance to get any impression of her, considering Elmer was yelling his face off at us, and just about everyone was arguing," Logan reminded him.

"Hmm."

Logan added the butter, then got to stirring some more, a

slow smile forming on his lips as Garrett continued to ramble.

"See, after Elmer called us up, we hurried over. Weren't sure if you two were together, but wanted to help him out, at any rate. Adelaide was there too. Anyway, we got to looking around the property together. We were talking and... she's nice. So I was just wondering."

"Nice." Logan tossed another look at his brother as he moved the bowl over to the frying plan.

"Yeah, I like her. So what? You obviously enjoyed the company of that crazy sister of hers."

Defensiveness caused the smile to slip from Logan's lips.

"Frankie's not crazy."

Garrett shrugged.

"Yeah, fine. All I know is, you better be careful around her. You heard what Adelaide said."

Logan stopped moving. The knot in his belly was getting tighter and tighter.

"Yeah. And I heard what Frankie said too."

Garrett opened his mouth, then closed it before parting his lips again.

"Forget it. Knowing Elmer how I do, that girl's probably grounded or worse. But I'm planning on stopping in later today, just to see how they're all doing. Maybe get a chance to talk to Adelaide under different circumstances. You want me to put a good word in?"

Logan poured the batter onto the buttered pan into careful circles, a half-smile forming on his mouth at the idea of anyone trying to ground Frankie.

"And say what?" Logan asked.

"I don't know. That you're a good guy."

"Elmer won't buy that. He's never liked me," Logan muttered.

Only the sounds of pouring and simmering filled the kitchen as Garrett considered the truth in Logan's words.

"You know, you could've put in more of an effort," his brother chided him gently. Logan snorted.

"Never had a reason to."

That was part of it but only part and Garrett knew it. Logan just didn't do well with most people—couldn't talk to them nor did he want to. The few times he did put in an extra effort to try, they sensed that something was off and almost always reacted suspiciously. He just did his best to leave everyone alone.

"Well," Garrett said as he headed out the kitchen. "Now you have a reason."

He left, leaving all he'd said to swim around Logan's head along with everything else.

All Logan knew was that he had to finish the pancakes to get his brothers out of his hair.

After that, he could start to pick through all he'd learned the night before and decide what to make of it.

And then I've got to figure out how to see Frankie again without getting murdered by Elmer.

CHAPTER 11

Frankie

"Well, look who it is!"

The sound of Addy's happy tone caused Frankie to dart out of her room to see who was at the door. It took her seconds to realize that her sister wouldn't have sounded so pleased to see Logan and her fears were confirmed when she saw one of the other brothers standing on the porch.

While Frankie had sulked in bed and tested the window as a means of escape, Adelaide had apparently changed into something suitable. Frankie admitted her sister looked beautiful in a pair of jeans and crisp, white top.

"Howdy." Garrett took off his hat, giving Addy an adoring look that made Frankie affectionately nauseous.

There is definitely something there, she decided, casting aside her own heartache.

Turning her head away to hide her obvious smile, she flinched as she realized even her neck was sore. It made sense that her legs and arms were aching after climbing with Logan yesterday but it was odd that her entire body seemed to pain in the aftermath of their climb.

Wow. I really need to get more activity. This is embarrassing.

Uncle Elmer was outside, yelling at the chickens for some unknown transgression, otherwise Frankie knew he'd be seizing this opportunity to lay into Frankie again.

"How is Logan?" Frankie asked. No point in playing coy. "Your brother?"

Garrett tore his eyes off Adelaide with difficulty.

"He's all right. Bit grumpy. You?"

"I'm fine," Frankie declared. "Other than the fact that my uncle who has no sense of humor grounded me."

"Ah, did he now?" An odd expression twisted Garrett's mouth.

"You already knew?" Adelaide realized.

"Ah, well, you know your uncle, he's renowned for…" Garrett tried waving his hat around like the word was floating in the sky.

"Being a stubborn mule?" Frankie supplied. "Yeah, not surprising."

Frankie skirted past them and into the kitchen. To her mind, the only thing that was going to make that morning anything close to bearable was caffeine.

"Anyway, I'll leave y'all to it."

"Just wanted to stop in, make sure everything was okay," Garrett said, as if it were an alibi.

"Uh-huh." Frankie gestured to the back door. "You want to avoid Uncle Elmer long as possible, there's two old half-broken lawn chairs back there. Or you can start weeding the garden, get on his good side. And if you're particularly lucky, you might get treated to his theory on how gardening cures many of today's common ailments."

Frankie left them to make the final decision themselves. After coffee, her plan could be in motion. With both Adelaide and Uncle Elmer presumably occupied, her best chance to escape was now.

Maybe I'll even clean up the kitchen to appease the old goat.

She reminded herself not to forget about Gus.

Frankie Mills was no one's prisoner. Her uncle couldn't just ground her like she was a child.

Anyway, it was important for her to see Logan again. She had to explain the situation to him, about Andrew and how little that relationship had meant to her. Frankie wanted Logan to understand that things were so much different when she was with him, even if they barely knew one another.

And there was no way that Uncle Elmer and Addy were going to stop her.

As Frankie ate her way through one well-honeyed bowl of Honey Nut Cheerios after the next, pausing to take quick swigs of coffee, familiar voices seeped in through the kitchen curtains. Frankie peered out. Garrett and Adelaide had taken her up on her suggestion. They were on the rickety lawn chairs, chatting away.

Frankie chuckled to herself.

At least we didn't fall for the same Thatcher boy.

The thought stopped her smile instantly.

She hadn't really fallen for Logan…had she?

She gulped down the last spoonful of Cheerios, downing the remnants of her mug and rose to her feet. There was only one way to be certain. She needed to find Logan.

Frankie raced around, cleaning every dirty surface she saw. There wasn't a shortage of them; Uncle Elmer preferred yelling at the contestants on Jeopardy to cleaning his own house. He'd also probably relied on Aunt Frida to do all the cleaning.

As she polished a slightly rusty teapot, Frankie couldn't stifle the guilty pang.

She wondered if she wasn't being hard on Uncle Elmer.

He'd gone through a lot, lately, after all, losing Aunt Frida. Those two had been a pair.

Aunt Frida herself had been a character. She was the kind of cheery person who was almost always smiling—not in an annoying way. She had the contagious good humor that could coax a smile out of anyone in minutes. She was one of the few people Frankie had never heard Uncle Elmer snap at. Frankie remembered that the two of them used to do everything together—grocery shop, garden, crossword puzzles.

And now that she was gone.

Maybe the old bull has a reason to be so miserable.

A shiver went through Frankie.

It troubled her to think about someone being so intrinsic to you, so perfectly fitted together... and then losing them. She couldn't imagine how life would go on after that, how anyone could move forward.

Frankie shook her head.

Now wasn't the time for gloomy deliberations.

She'd cleaned the kitchen to shining, and by some miracle, neither Uncle Elmer nor Adelaide had yet stepped foot in the house. If she was going to make her move, now was the time.

No need to check on Adelaide and Garrett, Frankie could hear the low happy murmur of their voices from the kitchen.

Uncle Elmer, on the other hand...

Frankie peered out of the front door, right then left but there was no sign of him. She imagined that he was in the barn.

That was another thing Uncle Elmer had taken up since Aunt Frida passed. Suddenly, he hung out in the barn alone with the animals. He sat there, not saying anything, as if the animals could understand what he was going through better than any other person.

She made a mental note to check on Gus later. The

feline was lively and fatter already. Frankie hoped that meant he was starting to be able to fend for himself, at least partially.

It was sad, but today Uncle Elmer's barn habits would work out well for Frankie. She grabbed her tote and hurried off.

Behind her, she heard the creak of the barn door, and her whole body tensed up, ready for the shout: "JUST WHERE YOU THINK YER RACIN' OFF TO!"

But it never came. Throwing a look behind her, Frankie saw that the wind had only gusted the door open slightly but there was no Uncle Elmer.

She grinned, the sun shimmering on her skin. Its noontime height and brightness, the spotless blue of the sky, the postcard worthy view of the fields she raced past, it all made her feel like her life was pre-ordained. She felt, for a moment, like she was doing precisely what she was supposed to.

Enveloped by the warmth, the slight breeze, the hay-flecked air, Frankie barely noticed Logan until she almost barreled into him.

"Hey."

He grinned.

"Hey."

"Fancy meeting you here."

"I was on my way to see a girl."

"What a coincidence. I was on my way to see a boy."

They smiled foolishly at each other.

"I'm really sorry about last night," Frankie blurted out. "Uncle Elmer freaked out. And I'm sorry what Adelaide said…"

Logan shook his head.

"Don't be. It's like you said, neither of us meant for it to happen."

"But still," Frankie insisted. "I wanted you to know how great of a time I had last night. And I want to see you again."

A smile tugged at the corner of Logan's lips.

"You're seeing me."

"I am." Frankie's gaze dipped to his hand, where a blanket was tucked, and a basket. "What's that for?"

"A picnic. I was thinking…"

"Yes," Frankie interjected and they both laughed.

"You didn't even hear what I had planned," Logan teased but Frankie was sure she didn't care. She was already on board with whatever he had in mind. "Maybe plan was for us to climb all the way up the first Potest mountain without any belays or harnesses, then we get to eat some nice yummy mashed sardines."

Frankie laughed.

"You ever climb up it?" she asked.

"There's a first time for everything."

"As for mashed sardines." She crinkled her nose. "Is that really even a thing?"

"Don't know," Logan admitted. "Don't want to find out, either."

He hooked his arm through hers.

"Come on, I know a place."

The contact of his bare muscled arm against hers sent tingles through Frankie. She bit her lip to stop smiling. She was going to get a sore face at this rate.

"Do I get to find out what you did pack for the picnic?" she asked as they sailed across the Thatcher's property. From what she could see, it was gorgeous; long-spanning fields, luscious gardens, a dark wooden ranch that looked right out of a storybook.

"You'll see soon enough," Logan replied coyly.

"Hm," Frankie said. "Fine, then I won't tell you what I packed for our picnic."

"You knew?"

"Great minds think alike."

Frankie almost laughed aloud, relishing how easily it was to be with him. She felt like she trusted him already.

Be careful, Fran.

Frankie frowned at Adelaide's voice in her head.

"What is it?" Logan asked, noting the expression on her face. She thought quickly, not wanting to tell him the real thought in her head. Frankie sighed.

"My uncle tried grounding me. And my sister was all for it, too."

"Garrett said he'd probably try that. I figured I'd have to go to you, apologize to your uncle myself, see if there was any way I could make amends."

"Yeah, he probably would have just yelled at you and chased you away with a hoe," Frankie snickered, only half joking.

"Yeah. I figured that, too."

She glanced to him, startled.

"What?"

Logan's brow was pinched, his mouth bitter.

"Your uncle doesn't like me. Never has."

"But why?" She looked at him quizzically.

His mouth quirked with that for a few seconds, before he muttered, "We really have to go over this again?"

"Sorry. I just..." Frankie searched for the right words. "Find it so hard to believe that people wouldn't like you. Not if they knew you."

Logan's eyes opened up like a flower.

"That's the thing though. They don't. It's not like this with other people. I can't..." He sighed, exasperated. "Not with anyone else, but my Ma. She's gone now."

Frankie's hand flew to her mouth, her cheeks paling at the revelation.

"Oh gosh, I'm sorry."

He shook his head, smiling slightly.

"Not *gone* gone. Just away on a trip. I was being melodramatic, sorry."

"That still sucks," Frankie agreed. "Especially if she was the only person you really connected with."

They'd come to a stop, and it took Frankie a few seconds to realize why.

Logan had found the perfect spot for their picnic. There was a generous patch of shade under the willow tree, the little stream burbling a few meters off. Frankie wasn't sure she could have imagined a better area in her mind.

This is exactly what I had in mind by coming out here, she realized, happiness sparking through her.

Logan set up the blanket, plopped down the picnic basket before speaking.

"It was past time for her to leave, my ma. She's always wanted to go on an around-the-world trip, just put it off because… anyway, once my Pa passed, she finally had her chance."

Before Frankie could open her mouth, he lifted a hand.

"It's fine. She'll be back before I know it."

He said it with the conviction of someone reading the lines off a script.

"Anyway, you ready to eat?"

"Am I ever," Frankie agreed, glad for the change of subject. She felt like he was holding back something about his parents but she also couldn't bring herself to ask, like it was too personal still. Instead, she nodded toward the basket and Logan hurried to open it.

As soon as Logan lifted the basket's thatched lid, Frankie beamed at him, surprise and happiness overwhelming her.

"How'd you know?"

Logan just smiled.

"Seriously!" Frankie demanded, "I'm starting to wonder if you have a secret spy camera in my house or something."

"Nah." As Logan shook his head, the light caught on the sandy strands, making him glint with handsomeness. "Just something I remembered from years back. At the market, your Aunt Frida had the best pancakes going. Figured you might have a hankering for them now that she's not around to make them."

Frankie had already scooped up some warm goodness and taken a bite. A sigh slid out of her pancake filled mouth.

"Oh wow," she murmured. "These are…oh, wow."

"Yeah?"

"Definitely." Frankie grabbed another and began eating furiously, then paused. "Sorry, I'm a complete pig."

Logan laughed.

"No, please. Pig out. I made these for you, though I told my brothers it was actually for them."

Frankie peered into the packed Rubbermaid container.

"You must've made a lot."

Logan cocked his head at her.

"Why'd you think it took me so long to get to you?"

Because you weren't coming, Frankie thought, but didn't say.

"Listen." She swallowed the rest of the pancake, so she could speak freely. She needed to get it off her chest—the thing she kept avoiding bringing up, nervous it would spoil their easy conversation. "About what Adelaide said. It's not how it sounds. I broke up with Andrew before I came here. It's over."

Logan was nibbling on his own pancake, clearly not into it. His gaze cut into Frankie.

"Was it serious?"

"No—yes. Well, to him it was."

Logan's brows shifted.

"Yeah?"

"I kept trying to break up with him, but he kept convincing me to give him another chance. Plus, my family adored him and everyone kept telling me how lucky I was to have him." Frankie hung her head. "That was another reason I left. I wanted to get away from all the people trying to pressure me into what I was *supposed* to do, supposed to feel. Always feeling like I was coming up short, like there was something wrong with me for not wanting to live according to their idea of who I am. You know, all I'd need to do is say the world and I could have an upper management position at my Dad's company tomorrow."

Logan's head cocked the other way.

"Yeah?"

"Yeah. The starting base salary is 80K, plus benefits. A perfect gig—if I wanted it. Same went for Andrew. He had the looks, the job, the friends. Perfect man—if I'd wanted him."

Frankie's hand flopped in her lap.

"That was just the thing, though. I didn't want any of it – not the job, and definitely not him. I didn't know what I wanted. I still don't. But I knew that I didn't want that." She sighed. "Am I making any sense at all?"

"Yeah, actually." Logan was looking at her in a new way. He took her hand. "Makes complete sense. It's how I feel every day. Like something's off."

His gaze was off in the distance.

"The only time I feel myself is when I'm climbing and when…"

"I'm with you," Frankie finished for him.

Their eyes met.

An eternity came and went in the gaze they held. The stream burbled, the wind whispered on her cheek, and Frankie couldn't have looked away if she wanted to.

His gaze fell to her lips.

All of her burned, buzzed with his touch, his hand, his nearness. His scent, like deep in the woods and something tempting she couldn't place. His advancing nearness, closer and closer and closer, eyes closing—

"Hate to break up the lovefest, but we have one angry farmer with a pitchfork headed here in five, so I suggest you two set yourself up a little more appropriately."

Frankie's eyes flew open.

One of Logan twin brothers stood before them, wagging a scolding finger.

"Seriously." The other twin looked genuinely concerned as he joined the pair, hands shoved in his pockets, mouth pulled off to the side. "Garrett just called us. Elmer is on his way and he is *not* happy."

CHAPTER 12

Logan

Logan scrambled away from Frankie as she did the same.

He cut a glare to Chance, who shrugged nonchalantly.

"Don't shoot the messenger."

"Couldn't you have told Garrett that we weren't here?" Logan growled. His brother didn't need to tell Logan what he'd already figured out. Their spot by the tree was clearly visible from the ranch and his brother had sold him out to Garrett.

Chance flung a scandalized hand to his chest.

"You expect me to lie to my own flesh and blood? Me? No, I couldn't find it in my heart to do so."

"You had no problems doing it when you were running off to visit Mary, or whatever your girl of the week was called."

The flashing in Chance's eyes changed.

"Listen, you're just lucky we ran out here to warn you instead of letting Elmer find ya'll in whatever state–"

"Guys," Chase interjected.

"We aren't hurting anyone," Logan said. "We're barely even touching."

Chance's lashes flickered.

"Yeah, but we both know Elmer wouldn't see it that way."

"*Guys*," Chase growled with more insistence.

"Oh, whatever to Uncle Elmer," Frankie declared. "He's not my boss. Forget about him."

Chance regarded Frankie approvingly, a smile curling up the corners of his lips as his gaze flicked back to Logan.

"Well, well, well, brother. She's a real spitfire, that one. I can see what you see in her." He winked back at her. "If you get bored of my brother, there's other Thatchers who'd love a chance, too."

Logan saw red. For a second, he had flash after flash, Chance with one giggly adoring girlfriend after another, girls in school who'd never talked to Logan, pulling him aside begging for favor with his charming, charismatic brother. It was always Chance.

Chance and Frankie? Over my dead body.

"Don't you talk to her," Logan hissed with more malice than he thought he possessed.

Chance's hands flew up, eyes widening with amused surprise.

"Whoa there, lover boy!"

"Guys!" Chase was practically yelling now. "He's close."

"I don't care," Frankie snapped. "Let him come. I'm not going home with him and that's final."

"And you lay off," Logan spat at Chance. "Just this once, for this one time, could you not…"

He trailed off, surprised at himself to hear the venom in his voice. The twins were too, their eyes an identical huge size.

He'd never spoken to Chance or any of the brothers like

that before. For years, he'd just borne the brunt of their snide jabs and 'joking' with silence, not wanting to get into it, not wanting to bother.

Maybe that's because I've never had anything to protect before.

"You think you're such a hotshot?" Chance had an ugly look on his face as he stabbed a finger back at the pens. "Why not Superman over there and take a ride on Joan?"

There was silence as Logan thought it over. He could feel Frankie's eyes on him as he mulled over the thought.

"Don't," Chase said quickly, elbowing Chance as he realized that Logan was thinking about it. "Ignore this joker. You know what Joan's like."

Logan did, all too well. The new horse Chance had bought on a whim and against their mother's advice, was wild. She was half mad with energy which was why she'd been named after Joan of Arc. It had been the last animal to join the farm before Pa had passed and sometimes, Logan felt like his father's spirit had possessed the unruly beast.

Logan knew the smart thing to do, what was expected of him.

But he was tired of it of always turning the other cheeks, of playing into Chance's hand,

Yes, big bro, no, big bro, whatever you say, big bro. Yes, I guess I'm just a scaredy-cat of the big bad wild horsy, big bro.

Not today. Not this time.

He look at Chance head-on.

"Yeah, all right. Think I'll give it a go."

Chance laughed derisively.

"For real? Wow, this chick has turned your brain to mashed potatoes even more than I thought."

"Leave him alone," Frankie snapped, suddenly on her feet as she read the tension fully.

"It's fine." Logan stood up, still maintaining eye contact with his brother. "He's used to me taking it."

"Logan, think this through," Chase said carefully. "You know Chance is just being an idiot. You leave that horse where it belongs—in the pen."

By now, Logan could see the small jellybean form of Elmer getting bigger, with two thinner bean forms behind.

They're all coming. It's now or never.

He could see Frankie looking at him with wide eyes.

"I'm doing it," Logan said but he wondered if he was speaking more to himself or the others.

Chance whistled in disbelief.

"There we have it! America's top idiot, signing up for his own funeral."

Logan looked at him hard.

"You don't get it, do you?"

Chance smirked with a waggle of his eyebrows Frankie's way, like he and her were in this together.

"No, Logey boy, can't say that I'm grasping your special brand of stupid."

Logan advanced so that he was nearly nose-to-nose with Chance.

"It's not about me taming the wild horse. It's about me going there and trying, even though I'm scared."

"Well at least you have that baseline of sense–"

"Me going there and doing it, knowing full well I might fail. Knowing full well I probably will. That's what true bravery is. That's what you've never understood. You, who only enrolls into competitions and picks fights you know you'll win."

Logan stomped towards the pen, he heard Chance's sarcastic slow clap behind him, and Frankie saying something else. Chase called after him. But Logan wasn't listening. He was focused fully on the task ahead, even though his heart was in his throat.

This wasn't about them, this was about him doing what

he was long overdue to do, facing what scared him the most. Being with Frankie had shown him that he had the capability to do that.

As he strode towards the pen, Frankie ran to keep up with him.

"Are they exaggerating how crazy this horse is?" she demanded warily. Logan nodded in the direction of the horse.

"You can see for yourself."

As they advanced, the brown horse whinnied and began racing in a wide frantic circle. Frankie exhaled sharply, her hand jumping to his.

"Logan, do you really have to?"

"Yes." He squeezed her hand. "I'm sorry."

She nodded, squeezed his, then let it go.

"Then kill it, babe."

Her 'babe' coated him with the last courage he'd been missing. Logan glided to the pen and threw open the door before he could change his mind.

Joan froze.

She would've been a beautiful horse, in different circumstances, with her gold-brown mane, a white star on the forehead, and white tail.

Now, she regarded him with a steady, deadly stare.

Logan took a breath, then walked on forward, his insides quivering with the movement.

Here goes everything.

As a rancher's boy, Logan knew that horses were the most perceptive domestic animals in the world. If Logan stayed calm, it was that much more likely that Joan would too. Even if, after months of the twins and Garrett's taming attempts, she was as wild as the day they unleashed her in her pen.

First Logan approached her from the front slowly, arm out.

"There, it's okay. It's me."

He considered that maybe Joan wasn't as wild as she was misunderstood.

The equine pawed the ground, then paused, nickered softly.

"It's okay." Logan put a hand on her muzzle. "We're going to do this, together."

Logan paused to conjure up memories of Pa, telling him about wild horse taming. Logan had shown an aptitude when he was younger, for a while. After what happened, the haze had descended, and Pa had never bothered with Logan again.

Maybe the knowledge is still there, tucked away. Maybe I can do this.

Logan kept one hand on Joan's muzzle, looked deep in her eyes.

"You ready?"

Another nicker, softer this time. Logan stroked his hand along.

"Right. Let's do this."

That was it, his cue to stride over to Joan's back, hook a leg up and get on.

His first mouthful of fresh air, he noticed how high he was, how clear the air was. He stroked Joan's mane and then reality came barging on in.

"My Lord, it's a miracle!" Chance cried, throwing out both hands, from beyond the pen.

"Are you crazy?" Garrett barked. "Get down from there!"

By now, he, Adelaide and Elmer had caught up. Elmer seemed oddly pleased.

"Let the boy prove himself," the old man cawed in a way that Logan felt was meant to be condescending.

"You can do it!" Frankie cried.

Joan had noticed the others too, and she didn't like it one bit. She unleased a sharp whine, then a jolt that sent Logan's whole body shaking. She pawed the ground and began running in her sharp usual circles.

A sharp whistle.

"Oy, not such a sure thing now, eh Logey boy?"

Logan didn't need to look to see who it was. There was only one of his brothers who would be so mocking. He didn't have time for that anyway. At the rate Joan was trotting in her frantic circles, he wouldn't be able to stay on for much longer.

He enmeshed his fingers into her mane, patted her neck.

"Come on. Ignore them. We can do this," he murmured, trying to placate the beast.

Get off now, while you still can.

His body was tensed with his instinct warning him off the horse. He could feel six pairs of eyes glued on his every move, expecting him to fail, expecting him to give up.

Time slowed but his thoughts bubbled.

He was reminded of climbing then, at the top of a tricky pass. How many times had he wanted to give up but wasn't that the best time to keep going?

To him, this was the same.

Logan tightened his hold on Joan's mane.

"I'm staying."

He said it as much for himself as for her. He almost missed the creaking sound behind him, his concentration fixed on the animal.

"Come on, Logan! I can distract her while you get off." It was Garrett, grim-faced, wagging a carrot inside the pen. Logan shook his head, eyes narrowing. He repositioned his thighs on Joan's back.

"Sorry Garrett. I can't do that."

He wasn't going to give up. Not this time.

He leaned in, close to Joan's ear, whispered, "Why don't we show them what we've got?"

He gave her flank a light slap and they were off at a trot.

It was really happening.

Gone was Joan's nervous energy, her frantic circles. She ran back and forth, and back again, her gait smooth and steady. For a heartfelt moment, the mare almost felt tame, naturally ridden like she'd always done this.

"Let's see some stopping and cantering!"

Hands cupped around his mouth to carry his yell further, sitting on the pen fence, was Chance.

The abrupt loud cry sent Joan into a frenzy. She reared, and Logan scrambled to find a good handhold. When her hoofs slammed into the dirt once more, she was a different horse. She was feral again—and furious. She charged for the fence where Chance was sitting, as Logan struggled to veer her off course but the effort was futile.

"Gah!" Chance leapt out of the way to barely miss being trampled.

Joan was crashed through the fence. Logan crouched low, the impact almost jolting him to the ground.

"Come on," he murmured to her, his pulse roaring in his ears. "You're better than this. You're…"

He realized where she was heading and his pleas died on his lips, suddenly understanding her entirely. She was moving toward the mountain range.

Joan just wanted to be free. Wasn't that what Logan had strained for all his life? Wasn't that why he trekked out to the mountain at any chance he could? How would he like life in a pen?

"Logan! We're coming for you!" Garrett called from behind him.

A quick glance over his shoulder saw Garrett on his black stallion, the twins on their tawny mares.

Logan stroked along the side of Joan's head.

"This is it. We have to go back now. I'm sorry."

Joan snorted at his words, setting into a full gallop.

Garrett's stallion was faster, though. Already, he was nearly beside them, reaching out to Logan.

"Take my hand!"

Joan made a disapproving sound, and shifted. Logan's whole body was thrumming.

It was obvious what he should do: let his brother help him, save him, take Garrett's hand.

But all of him instinctively recoiled from the aid, as if his insides knew something he didn't.

Why didn't he want to return to safety?

He hadn't tamed the wild beast, not in the least. No, as they galloped through the fields, head back, country air filling his head, too fast for even the sun to catch up, Logan remembered why he'd loved riding, once upon a time. It was an entirely different kind of freedom.

He hadn't tamed the wild horse; in fact, the wild horse had made him wild.

"Logan!" Garrett hissed sharply, "What are you waiting for?"

The arm was still out, closer now. But it wouldn't be for long.

Do it

– don't.

You know it's the right thing. You have to

– no.

The back and forth might have continued in his head if Garrett hadn't joined his side and reached for Logan. Joan reared, giving Logan no other option but to cling to his brother's outstretched limb.

With one hand on and one hand off, there was no staying on her back and Logan was falling. Someone shouted and the horse whinnied. The ground rose up to meet him, claim him as his vision failed.

You'll thank me, one day, Logan heard from somewhere unidentifiable.

"Logan, Logan, you all right? You okay? Talk to me Logan!" Garrett shook him wildly.

Logan opened his eyes.

Everything was bright, slanting. The pain that started to claim him had faded away into the haze.

"Jesus, he okay?" Logan heard Chase's voice.

"Dang, if I'd had any idea he'd actually—" started Chance.

"Shut up," Garrett yelled, his tone laced with panic.

Logan didn't like this haze. It wasn't like the others which brought him out of reality. This was different, claiming his lower body somehow.

His voice ripped out of him from a place he couldn't understand.

"I can't feel my legs! I can't feel my legs!"

The haze was spreading to his vision as he flailed, closing his lids even as he fought to keep them open.

"Logan?" another voice cried out, one he both yearned for and dreaded to hear.

The haze overtook all of him now and Logan knew he had no choice but to succumb to it.

"Frankie?" he tried to whisper but it his voice was lost. His eyes were closed. The haze had won the battle.

CHAPTER 13

Logan

Beep-beep-beep
  Beep-beep-beep
  Beep-beep-beep

Logan's side ached. The fog was slowly lifting even though he still didn't quite understand what was happening.

Beep-beep-beep
  Beep-beep-beep
  Beep-beep-beep

Memories pranced around, recent and far gone, all swirling around in his head like a giant tumbleweed, tangled and messy.

There had been a doctor with lash-less pea-green eyes and burnt red cheekbones. He leaned over Logan's face in a strange blur, his voice harsh and loud. A more familiar voice piped through, making proclamations as he stayed hidden in the spice cupboard and said hello to the haze as it befell him. In this faded recollection, the entire family was there, cowering as teacups smashed against the wall. He saw her again but it was for the first time.

Her hair the same intensity as red swirls of the wild strawberry jam he put on his toast every morning, eyes so blue, they must have taken the sky's pigment for themselves.

Lips curled into a sly, beam as if she knew something that Logan didn't and oh, how he wanted to know.

She sat with her legs swinging haphazardly, leaning forward just enough to make him question what she was doing there—was she about to say hello or spring to her feet and walk away without a word?

And now...

"Frankie?" Logan murmured, his voice scratchy. He felt like he had swallowed sandpaper. Slowly, painfully, he managed to open his eyes.

I'm in a hospital.

"Hello to you too," Chance chirped.

Logan closed his eyes.

"You! Get *out*," Garrett snapped at the twin. Logan heard slight grumbling but the shuffle of feet as Chance moved to oblige.

"Logan, we're sorry." Chase spoke now. "I'm sorry. We should've never let you—"

Logan shook his head, strained his eyes back open.

"It's not your fault."

"If Chance wasn't such an idiot—" Garrett began.

"My fault," Logan muttered, even though his mouth was stuffed full of cotton.

Suddenly, he remembered the horse, the fall.

"My legs?" he whispered.

Sorrow wiped the rage clean off Garrett's face. He looked away and the expression on his brother's face told Logan everything he needed to know.

"The doctor doesn't... he's being conservative," Garrett said falteringly. "But he still doesn't know for sure."

Logan nodded again, and yawned. The haze was settling back in, blocking out the reality again, as it always did when things got too tough.

"Thanks for... for..." he started but his eyes began to close and his mind was drifting away.

They still don't know, he thought irrelevantly. *No one knows but this isn't the time.*

The haze carried him along until time lost all meaning.

He floated through doctors who proclaimed, and nurses who chatted. Familiar voices spoke to him but he wasn't there.

Logan wasn't anywhere.

∼

"You're back!"

Chase dropped the Rodeo News magazine he was reading to the floor as he leapt up, his face etched in concern.

Logan blinked at him.

"How you feeling?" Garrett asked, while Chance stayed sulking in the corner with his phone.

Logan found his voice and tested it,

"Okay."

It sounded like endoscopes and tapioca pudding in alarming quantities.

"My legs?" Logan asked weakly.

"Your legs will be fine, the doctor thinks." There was a hopeful, happy note in Garrett's voice that hadn't been there before. "You'll just need to do a lot of physical therapy and be super careful."

"And climbing?"

His brothers stared at him with equal dubiousness.

"We didn't ask." Chase said curtly.

Garrett frowned at his brother before turning his attention back to Logan.

"The doctor did say that you won't be able to do any strenuous activities for most likely at least a month, maybe even months."

Garrett eyed him meaningfully.

So no climbing for months. No nothing but...

"And Frankie?" he mumbled.

"You just missed her." Logan couldn't read the expression on Garrett's face. "She's come by every day for hours, as often as she can. Elmer is doing his best to keep her back at the farm but that doesn't stop her."

"Looks like you've got a keeper there, Logey," Chance sneered.

"Shut up, Chance!" Garrett and Chase chorused, giving Chance a scathing look.

Logan smiled. The blanket of weariness that had momentarily lifted was descending once again.

The next time he was roused from the depth, he was only half awake.

"What about Ma?" someone murmured in a voice so low, Logan couldn't identify who it was. "We weren't sure, if you'd want us to…"

"No," Logan mumbled back. "No. Don't tell her. Don't ruin her trip."

There were several more ins and outs, the painkillers and hazes keeping him in and out of consciousness but when he woke again, he smelled her before he laid eyes on her.

Slowly, his lids parted and he stared at her, taking in the sight with eager eyes.

The red-red hair, the overalls, and freckled snub nose.

"Frankie."

She leapt up from the chair, dropping her book on the floor.

"You're awake!"

"I am. For now."

For the first time, he felt genuinely awake, not ready to succumb into darkness again.

"It's good to sleep," Frankie said quietly. Her blue eyes skidded over his face, scanning it but for what?

"I'm sorry," she burst out, crouching to pick up her book. "About the whole Uncle Elmer thing and everything. I never should've let you..."

Logan shook his head, turned away.

"It wasn't your decision to make."

"But still, I wish I'd just have done *something*."

"What? Stopped me from making an idiot of myself?"

That's what he had done, after all.

So much for impressing the girl.

"I thought what you did was very brave." Frankie's voice was quietly defiant. "Your brothers told me afterwards about how you hadn't had much experience with horses for a while now."

Yeah, I bet they did.

"Brave and stupid aren't mutually exclusive." Logan's head hurt. "And now I'm going to have to pay the price. No climbing, no anything, for months."

Frankie's jaw set.

"With physical therapy, the doctor said you'll be fine."

"I know what he said. Truth is, he doesn't know. I do. The one thing I care about most in life has just been ripped away from me."

Frankie paused, as though waiting for something more. She stared at him plaintively, coaxing more out of him but when he didn't say anything else, she exhaled.

"Sounds like you want to be alone," she murmured, her

eyes willing him to argue her assessment but he couldn't. She was right. He did want to be left alone in his misery, to wallow and overthink as always.

Logan watched her go as he wondered blithely if he had suffered a brain injury too. He'd wanted nothing more than to see her and now, he'd just let her walk out the door—again.

Too late, he called out, "No, wait! Frankie, wait!"

Frankie's frowning face appeared around the door but she didn't make any move to enter.

"I mean it, Logan. If you don't want me here, then just tell me to go away and let you feel sorry for yourself in peace." She turned to regard him halfway. "Yes, what happened to you is horrible, and not fair. I'm so so sorry it did."

Her face crumpled, then hardened.

"But I didn't think you were the type to lose hope as soon as things gets bad. I don't know, maybe I'm wrong." Her words settled in his gut, hard and horrible. "Then again, maybe you are."

When he spoke, his voice was hoarse and ugly.

"I don't know anymore." Her mouth quivered, but he kept going, trying to explain it before he could lose his nerve. "Growing up, getting away to climb was the one thing that kept me going. The one thing. And now... what do I have left? What is there?"

Cheeks pinked, Frankie spun to face him, eyes flashing as the heaviness of his words struck her. Her mouth parted in disbelief.

"You have me. Or *had*, anyway."

She didn't give him a chance to respond, to explain himself as she stormed out the door again.

"No! Wait—!"

But Logan was held into the bed by an inordinate amount of tubes, beeps, tapes.

THE COWBOY'S ONE AND ONLY

And by legs that didn't quite work.

No.

He wouldn't let this be taken from him too.

He wouldn't let them keep him from her.

Amid the rips and beeps, he lurched after her, grabbing on anything nearby to keep from falling over. There was a pair of crutches by the door.

He was tottered through it with them—almost falling on his face. He found his footing at the last second, holding onto the walls to keep him from falling over.

"Frankie!"

She stopped, turning to gape at him.

"What are you doing?" she gasped, spinning back toward him.

"Coming to tell you that I've been an idiot. To ask you to come back."

"Logan." A strong-jawed nurse hustled in front of him, her lantern chin set at a dangerous angle. "You have to go back to your room."

Logan looked past her, set his eyes on the only thing that mattered.

"Frankie. Please."

She bit her lip, then nodded, following after them.

"Fine."

He let the nurse bustle him back to his bed, and reattach the army of tubes to him, as Frankie joined them inside.

"Are you insane?" Frankie demanded, as soon as the nurse had left and the door had shut behind her.

"Maybe." Logan sat there, mulling it over. "But I actually feel kind of good."

Frankie advanced tentatively.

"What, really?"

Logan bobbed his head.

113

"I don't know, maybe it's just an adrenaline rush from chasing you, but I feel pretty good now."

Frankie spun a red curl round her finger.

"Your brothers said there's still a few more days before you're discharged. The doctor is playing it safe."

Logan's gaze wandered to the window, which didn't offer him an escape: a charming view of a blah-grey office wall opposite.

"I don't need to be here anymore."

His legs were clearly wrecked, and he wasn't an expert in handling crutches, but his head was clearer than it had been since he'd arrived.

Maybe it was Frankie being there or just time or the cocktail of fiddling and drugs the hospital had given him, all he knew was, for the first time since the accident, he felt awake. Alive.

Frankie sat down on a plastic chair in the corner, hands folded, regarding him with a look that was like a pop quiz.

"Are you sure?"

Logan used the bed and his stronger leg to come to a tottering standing position. He kept his hold on the bed, and squared his shoulders.

Inhaled.

Exhaled.

Waited.

Realized.

"Yeah, I am actually," he told her and he meant it.

Frankie nodded to herself for a second, then rose.

"I'm going to come back tonight. We'll see how you feel then, and if you still feel great, then…" She tightened her lips together, set off for the door. "Then we'll see."

"Wait. What?" Logan protested. "We barely got to talk. I haven't found out… how are you? How's Gus? How's everyone?"

Frankie smiled.

"I'm all right. Uncle Elmer is keeping me busy, as you can imagine. Adelaide and Garrett are quite the item, they're going on dates now already. Gus is grand, too—your brother is letting him live on your property with the goats. They're all thick as thieves already."

Logan chuckled, imaging the cat with Forti.

"I'll bet. Can't wait to see that."

"And you will." Frankie's smile had switched to a careful look. "Only, I don't know if we should push it yet, Logan. You're doing so much better, and if the doctor says…"

"Didn't the doctor mistake me for someone who'd gotten shot during a failed heist because our charts got mixed up?" Logan surprised by his own words.

Frankie giggled, although her eyes were goggled on him.

"You remember that?"

Logan smiled, shrugged.

"Guess I do. Point is, what the doctor says isn't law. Doctors can make mistakes too. The third leading cause of death in the US is due to doctor and nurse error."

Frankie gave him a strange look and Logan shook his head.

"Never mind," he said quickly, "Just a project I did in high school. Point is, I know how I'm feeling. I'm going to ask them if I can go soon; let's see what they say."

That seemed to relieve Frankie a bit.

"All right. Sounds like a good idea to me, too. See you later, Logan."

"See you, Frankie."

It was only once she was gone that Logan realized the emptiness she'd left in her wake.

He asked the nurses about being discharged but they only smiled colorlessly at him, assuring him that he'd be out of there before he knew it.

Only once they left his room did Logan smile too.

He had a good feeling that he was going home soon.

～

Even though he was napping, as soon as Frankie stepped into the room, Logan knew.

The air changed, became more charged and his eyes opened immediately.

"Whoa sleepyhead." Frankie had on a dark hoodie and a grin that liked to cause trouble. "You sure you up for this?"

"For what? You didn't exactly tell me what was going on," Logan pointed out.

"Oh, you know." Frankie's face was a study of innocence now. "Just some sightseeing. A field trip."

"You mean an escape."

"Shh!"

Logan smirked. "The nurses out there are more concerned with eating donuts and swapping ex-husband sob stories than me, trust me."

Frankie's hand flew to her mouth.

"The witches!"

Logan shrugged.

"Just tell them you're taking me to the Starbucks downstairs, and we'll be right back."

"So we're really doing this?" Frankie said.

"I thought that's why you came."

"Did it ever occur to you that I may want to just see you, bedridden or not?"

"Ah."

"All right. Dang it, let's do it. You need help with the crutches?" She brought them over to where he was sitting.

"I'll be good." He nodded firmly. "And one more thing."

Frankie lifted a plastic bag he hadn't noticed.

"Brought you some clothes. Lucky for you, Uncle Elmer is trim in the legs and big in the belly. So you'll be sporting some pretty wonky clothes. Such is the price of freedom."

"Works for me," Logan laughed. Frankie really had thought of everything. "Let's do this."

CHAPTER 14

Frankie

Leaving was easier than they'd expected. No one was at the nurses station, although further down the hall they could hear giggling and shushing from the congregant of medical staff.

In minutes, they were out of the ward, in the hallway, in the elevator. Logan moved awkwardly on the crutches, still not used to them, although he refused any help when Frankie offered.

He was quick changing in the bathroom and soon, they were on their way out of the hospital.

Frankie's heart only stopped skipping when they stepped outside and the electric doors clanged slowly behind them.

"There." She spun to grin at Logan. "Free as birds. Now, what do you want to do?"

Logan eyed her, slightly stunned. He clearly hadn't thought that far ahead.

"Thought you'd just want to..." he began.

"Go back to the ranch?" Frankie wrinkled her nose. "I mean, we could, make up some story about how evil the nurses were—not that it would be much of a lie. I heard some of them giggling about missed medications but we're in town already. So…"

Her eyes trailed outwardly as if to say, "the world is our oyster."

"Hm." Logan's gaze wandered in another direction. "All right. Want to go to Wallaby's?"

"The restaurant?"

"Yeah. Most popular one in town."

"Okay. You good to make it?"

"Sure."

It wasn't the loudest proclamation of confidence that Frankie had ever heard but it beat standing in front of the hospital, mulling over their options.

"All right," Frankie peered in the direction Logan was looking. "Is it far? I could order us a cab."

Logan shook his head, pointed one way with his crutch.

"It's super. Three-minute walk or less."

"Sounds good." Frankie held out her arm. Logan stared at her.

She let it drop, catching the determination in his face.

"Sorry. It wasn't because…"

She trailed off, feeling stupid. She had been about to say something else. She was about to say that she hadn't done it because of his legs but then he would think she was only trying to touch him.

What's wrong with that? A small voice cried out to her but she didn't offer her arm again.

As they walked, neither spoke. It couldn't have been three minutes, in all the time it gave Frankie to rethink their decision.

This might not be such a good idea.

However, the fake-wood exterior and the rusty Wallaby's sign were coming into view, giving her little time to voice her reservations. At the door, Logan held it open for her.

"You didn't have to do that," she said, although she was smiling.

"I'm not that bad off," he replied, a slight edge to his voice. They stopped in the entranceway and Logan stared at her.

"What?" Frankie demanded, her own nerves frazzled.

"If you're going to tiptoe around me like I'm some invalid—"

"Then what?" Frankie interjected, "You'll just limp on home?"

Logan balked at her tone.

"Anyway," she continued, "you're getting angry over nothing. I'm not tiptoeing around you. At all. Hello! I just helped you escape from a hospital where you were supposed to stay for three more days."

Logan swallowed, a look of contrition falling over his face.

"Right. Sorry. Think I'm just…"

"A bit messed up from those heavy meds you were on?" she offered.

Logan bobbed his head, a half-smile forming on his face.

"Probably, yeah. About those…"

Frankie pulled out a small brown paper bag and shook it.

"They already had a bunch packed away for home."

Logan raked a hand through his hair.

"Jeez. I *am* sorry, Frankie."

Frankie tried to smile, but ended up just not scowling.

"Let's just get some food. We're probably both starving."

The interior didn't scream "fine dining." Mounted on the wall were the heads of a hairy bison, a balding deer and a cross-eyed skunk who looked about as happy to be there as Frankie was.

They had barely taken their seats when a waitress with two bobbing wine-colored pigtails assaulted them.

"Hiya, how can I help y'all? Ya'll want any of our apps on special—BBQ pig's tails, mac and cheese with extra Sriracha, pierogis with bacon bits—"

"No," Frankie told her, cutting off her seasoned spiel. "We'd like to look at a menu first, please."

The waitress' premade smile froze but she nodded, sauntering away without another word.

Frankie glanced to Logan, but his face was hard to read.

"Yep," he said. "All the girls in my school just about loved this place."

"So what?" she demanded with an unreasonable defensively. "You figured I'd *love* this crap place as much as they did, is that it?"

Logan's eyebrows leapt, then lowered.

"No, I didn't mean that... I just... don't know what girls like, so figured I'd try this."

"Oh, okay." Instantly, she felt ashamed of herself. "Sorry, I just...

"Don't worry about it. I've been a bit of a jerk these past few hours," Logan said quickly and Frankie sighed.

"You were injured," Frankie argued, unsure what excuse she had to give.

"Still," Logan muttered. "You've the one who's been the most decent to me through this whole thing. I shouldn't be jumping down your throat."

"Anyway." He picked up a napkin, gave it to her, picked up another, then waved it. "Enough about me. How are you doing? And how did you even pull this off anyway?"

Frankie grinned.

"My story is that I'm currently at the library Skyping with my parents. It's unbelievable that in this day and age, someone in America doesn't have Wi-Fi."

Logan laughed.

"You'd be surprised how many people don't have internet around here," he replied. "So you've already caught up enough with your parents then?"

Frankie's head jerked up and she paled slightly.

"No, I..." Frankie trailed off. She hadn't planned on having this conversation. "I'm actually enjoying getting some space from them."

"Space can be good," Logan agreed.

"I mean, it probably makes me sound totally soulless and uncaring, and I do miss them, just, it can get to be a bit much, you know?" Frankie was beginning to wonder who she was trying to convince. "They've always known exactly what they've wanted, so they figure if I don't it's because *they* know what I want."

Frankie picked up her napkin and let it fall.

"They're so intent on me being who they think I should be, that they don't give me space for who I am." She paused to take a breath. "Does that make any sense?"

Logan didn't need to answer, the look in his eyes did.

"I've felt that way my whole life," Logan confessed and something swelled in Frankie that she hadn't realized was low and ducking.

The evergreens of his eyes held something else too, something happy and surprised and furtive at finding recognition in another.

Under the table, Frankie felt his foot fall beside hers.

The wooden front door banged open, bringing with it a tempting gust of fresh air.

"It's a sign," Frankie joked.

"To get out of here." Logan's gaze was already out the door. "Want to?"

"Seriously?"

"Seriously." He made a faux-serious face. "Unless you'd rather have some BBQ pig's tails."

"Oh *no*." Frankie said sarcastically, as she was grinning. "Guess I'll have to find a way to live with that."

This time, Logan was the one who held out his arm. The gesture told her everything and without hesitating, Frankie took it, the two disappearing out the door.

Outside, they didn't make fast progress, with Logan still figuring out the nuances of using crutches, but they made do. Frankie got to see that the main part of downtown was bigger and more interesting than she'd originally realized.

"Have to say," she told Logan, stopping to pat one of the vibrantly painted mailboxes. "Your mailboxes put ours to shame."

"Oh yeah?" Logan smirked. "I thought all mailboxes were painted with scenes from Vimy's Ridge."

"That's Vimy's Ridge?" Frankie shook her head, peering closer at the little scene painted in a sharp realist style with bright splashes of red, yellow and blue. "Nah, that's supposed to be the Battle of Dieppe, isn't it?"

Logan pointed at a little block of writing off to the side of the box.

"The caption would beg to differ."

Frankie leaned in to read the small Arial-style font, 'A scene from Vimy's Ridge, soldiers storming the ridge'.

"All right, all right." She laughed, her gaze already moving on down the street, to the next mailbox. "Let's see what this one is then!"

That started their mailbox pilgrimage, sending them wandering from street to street, taking breaks for Logan's legs as they admired the colorfully decorated mailboxes.

"Gorgeous," Frankie murmured, her eyes no longer on the painted image of Pearl Harbor. Her eyes were on the necklace in the shop window, a rose-gold one with a blue stone inlay.

"Want to try it on?" Logan asked, studying her face with an admiring expression but Frankie was too transfixed to notice much else but the necklace before her.

"Oh no." Frankie laughed a little even though she was lying. "The place probably isn't even open and—"

"Howard Ang Collectibles is open late," Logan interrupted.

Frankie paused, then shrugged.

"All right then."

Inside, they had to navigate their way through a baffling but beautiful assortment of knick-knacks. There was everything from a tin monkey with penny-sized drums and a red sombrero to a life-size baby elephant made of pure gold to a cinnamon-smelling chair the size of a car, carved from a single piece of wood. They finally located Howard Ang himself in the back of all the clutter. He was a compact Asian man with disapproving lip corners but merry eyes.

"Could my friend try on the necklace in your display?" Logan wondered. Howard nodded eagerly and moved to remove the piece from the front window. Less than a minute later, the cool links of the necklace sat around Frankie's upper collarbone and she was holding a seashell mirror to gauge her reflection.

"Oh, *wow*," she breathed, her face etched with pleasure.

She somehow felt like she wasn't looking at herself in the glass. She had transformed into an older, classier version of herself, one with bluer eyes and an almost regal bearing about her.

How can one little piece of jewelry change someone so much?

"I don't even want to look at the price," she confessed, prying her eyes off her reflection with difficulty. She was sure she'd never been so struck by an ornament before but there was just something about it…

"Then don't." Logan shrugged a shoulder. "I'll get it."

"Don't be silly," Frankie said, reaching to unclasp the necklace from her neck.

I shouldn't have tried it on.

"I'm not being silly. I want to buy it for you."

"Logan—"

"Let me do this."

"But you don't even know how much it is! It could be— "

Frankie felt the brush of his fingertips, then the necklace moved. Gooseflesh exploded over her flesh at the feel of his hands on her skin.

"It's $76. There."

"That's too much," Frankie said shortly.

"You know it's not."

She was quiet. Different thoughts shot through her mind.

"Logan…"

But he was already on his way to the cash register with the necklace in one hand and a wave. "Too late."

Next thing she knew, he was back, his face shining.

"I'm serious." Frankie fought the encroaching smile on her face with a firm frown. "I'm paying you back."

"And I'm serious too." Logan's easy smile wasn't budging. "This is a gift. It looks perfect on you."

He went over to drape it around her neck again and Frankie relished his nearness.

"Thank you," she murmured, conscious of how close he was to her.

She threw her arms around him, keeping her body stiff, her thoughts severe. If she let the gratitude she felt swelling through her overwhelm her, if she let herself press her body to him how she wanted to…

She drew back with difficulty.

"Let's go?"

Logan opened the door for her.

"Let's go."

Outside, they were barely a few steps down the sidewalk, when something stopped them again. The sound of music wafted into their ears, causing Frankie to spin around.

"Hey,

Wait around the train station,

Waitin' for that train..."

"I know this song!" Frankie peered into the bar it was coming from. As if guided by the music, Frankie entered the tavern.

One step inside the dark, Jimi Hendrix-crooning warmth, she turned to see if Logan had followed. He was mere steps behind her and with a tilt of his head, he indicated a table at the back, and they sat down.

The music was entrancing.

It was no Jimi Hendrix, but the cover band on stage was doing it justice. Even the atmosphere felt new, although Frankie had seen live bands before. She could see the sweat roll down the sax player's face, smell the beer the waiter passed by their table to carry to the band, feel the wooden planks reverberate under her feet with the music.

She only snuck a nervous look at Logan once, wondering if he felt the music as deeply as she did.

When her gaze rested on him, eyes steady and intent on the stage, lips open ever-so-slightly, it was obvious. He got it, all right.

This time, the band played three songs before the server stopped by.

"Drinks?" he asked.

"Sure," Frankie agreed. "What kind of tea do you have?"

"The non-alcoholic kind." The waiter winked, as if it were a joke, a gentle call out to their age.

"Perfect. I'll have mint, please," Frankie smiled.

"Me too," Logan added.

"Right, two teas." The waiter's thin mouth curved around the 'teas' as though it was a new word. "That everything?"

"Yep," Logan said, "thanks."

And then the waiter left and they were eyeing each other carefully.

"You don't drink?" Logan asked. Frankie shook her head.

"No, you?"

"Nope." There was a finality about the way he said it that made her want to know more.

"Why not?"

Logan paused for a moment and Frankie thought he might not answer but to her surprise, he did.

"Saw what it did to my Pa, early on." Logan shook his head, upper lip curling. "Knew I didn't want any part of what that does, ever."

"Ah." Frankie wasn't sure what to say that. Only her hand ached to grab his, but it wasn't the time.

A new band was preparing to start, was tuning their instruments with fitful notes and bursts of chords.

Logan's gaze had slung at her.

"Why don't you?"

"Didn't like how I behaved when I did drink." Frankie shrugged. "Way I figure, if I don't have the courage or smarts to do something sober, I definitely shouldn't be doing it drunk."

There's still one thing I don't have the courage to do...

"Here's to that." Logan raised a glass of water, one that Frankie hadn't even noticed was on the table. She picked up hers too, and their glasses clinked.

"To being sober and happy with nothing to regret," she proposed.

Their gazes held as they sipped.

She marveled at how much different a couple hours had made in Logan. There was a glint in his eyes that hadn't been there in the hospital. He almost looked happy.

Under the table, Frankie could feel not just his foot, but his whole leg next to hers.

She tipped her head to his and said,

"This..." She paused, waiting for more words to come but they wouldn't. They all fell short of what she wanted to say. She opened her mouth again and cleared her throat. "Thank you."

Though it wasn't at all enough, even though it didn't begin to describe the absolute joy sparkling through her veins, Logan smiled.

They remained in that position, heads tilted together, legs resting as one, for one song after the next as the band continued to play and the tea flowed. It wasn't until the band began to pack up on stage that she reluctantly looked at her phone.

She had to check it several times, the numbers on the screen seemed so incongruous:

9 pm. Already?

She had a sense of déjà vu, remembering their night on the mountain and how quickly time seemed to pass when she was with Logan.

"I should be getting back home soon." Frankie felt like she had to rip the words out of her. They were the last things she wanted to say. "Otherwise we might have to endure Uncle Elmer Family Incident Number Two."

Logan sighed but nodded in agreement.

"You're right." Logan rose with a quick grab of his crutches and a nod. "I've got this."

"Logan!" Frankie protested.

"You rescued me from the hospital," Logan pointed out. "It's the least I can do."

"Still…"

Logan paused.

"Guess you're right," he said, pulling a face. "Seeing as the bill will be a *whole six dollars* with tip."

Frankie tried not to grin but failed.

"There. Glad we agreed."

On the way out, Frankie grabbed the bar's weekly schedule in the form of a pamphlet.

"Probably won't be back any time soon," she confessed to Logan's surprised look. "It's just to remember."

From there, time sped up again—only for a moment. They left the bar and moved a few steps, out of the light of the bar before stopping. Logan turned to her, taking the necklace in his hands as he pretended to study it before raising his eyes to look at her.

Everything slowed again.

"One souvenir's not enough for you?" His voice was low, his gaze dipping down to the pamphlet still clutched in her hand.

"Guess not." Frankie couldn't have faked a chuckle if she'd tried. Her heart was racing at his nearness. Her pulse overtook her body, everything else was fading except Logan and his scent.

Abruptly, gust of wind ripped the pamphlet away from Frankie.

"No!" she cried, reaching for it at the same time as Logan. And Logan was on the sidewalk, a sickening crunch breaking his fall.

A scream flew out of Frankie as she gawked at him in shock.

Logan waved the pamphlet in his hand with a grimace of victory.

"Relax. I got it."

Frankie couldn't remember how to smile, how to tear her

gaze off of the very wrong arrangement of his legs on the ground and what it meant. She tried to get past the incessant cries playing over and over in her head.

Oh. My. Gosh. No!

Her body suddenly unfroze and Frankie dove down to grab him by the arm.

"You okay? Logan, I'm so sorry, I'm such a klutz. But you shouldn't have done that, you could've…"

He was silent, breathing heavy.

"Logan?" Frankie said tentatively, all of her tensed with fear. "Are you…"

She trailed off, her voice cracking as she read the completely blank expression on his face.

"My leg," he murmured, his words barely a whisper. "I can't feel my leg."

CHAPTER 15

Logan

Tick-tock. Tick-tock. Tick-tock.

All of Logan ached to bash the grandfather clock's ever-ticking face but that was hardly an option. .

His legs were still numb blocks of nothing.

He swallowed, reminded himself and reminded himself to feel lucky.

He had managed to convince his brothers and Frankie not to take him back to the hospital even though he had a feeling that was where he was supposed to be.

Still, he didn't feel lucky.

He felt nothing.

Frankie sat on the loveseat, her face a turned-away mask of guilt. She'd given up trying to make conversation a while back.

If only I could explain...

A part of him had suspected this coming all along, the fall

after the rise, his comeuppance. With Frankie, it had been too good, he'd been too happy.

Nothing good lasts. You know that.

Logan closed his eyes.

He was grateful his brothers had finally left. He hadn't known how long he could bear it, the looks on their faces, the puzzlement. He could read their silent questions.

Why did you do this to yourself? Why take the risk?

They were the same questions that banged around in Logan's skull along with others.

Like when is the doctor going to show up? And how long is Frankie going to sit here before she figures it out?

∽

Logan watched as the doctor arrived in a clop of chunky kitten heels and a mustard tweed blazer that made Logan itch just looking at it. His brothers followed her in.

It took the chunky woman minutes to make her diagnosis and dole out Logan's sentence.

"Your legs are broken," she intoned flatly. "You'll be lucky if you walk in half a year."

What she didn't say—the one thing that mattered—was obvious.

You'll be lucky if you climb again.

Climbing.

The one thing. The *one thing* that had gotten Logan through his life had been ripped away.

As the haze descended fully, Logan caught a few more words.

"...physical therapy... may be longer... have to be vigilant... need to be more careful... do you understand?"

Only after a long silence, and the doctor repeating, "Logan?" did he understand that it was his cue to speak.

"I understand," he said dully even though he didn't, not really.

"Don't worry." It was Garrett, speaking with an optimism his grim jaw didn't have. "We'll help you with whatever you need."

"While you're healing, we can get you a chair," Chase cut in, trying to smile. "Mrs. O'Leary has the old rickety one from when she broke her hip, it'll probably do."

Frankie's round eyes were those of the lost. When she opened her mouth, nothing came out until she clamped them shut again.

They stared him, like a squashed fly on a slide.

"Logan," Garrett spoke carefully now, "Do you want us to stay?"

"No."

His brother nodded.

"Right. Well, we'll bring dinner over in a bit. And remember, if you need anything…"

"Got it."

Finally, they left. Only it wasn't better, it was worse.

She was still there, looking at him, expecting things he didn't have anymore.

Frankie stood by his side, as close as she dared.

"Logan… I'm so sorry… I feel so guilty. This is all my fault."

Tears rolled down her face.

All of him clenched. He ached to brush those tears aside, to brush her sadness and guilt aside, and tell her that it wasn't her fault, that everything would be fine.

But he didn't have it in him to lie to her anymore, to make believe he was different than he was. He didn't have it in him to pretend he was the kind of man who could be with a girl like her.

Logan only realized they'd been sitting there for some

time when she said, in a very different voice, "Do you want me to leave?"

All it took was a nod for her to go.

Logan was alone now but not entirely. He had his thoughts to keep him company. He was free to overthink and agonize over everything he'd ever done wrong.

Welcome to the next six months of your life, he thought grimly. He wondered if this was his punishment.

CHAPTER 16

Frankie

"Ugh!"

The barn rustled with the animals' grumblings in reaction to her exclamation. The pigs snorted —Daphne's loudest of all, the horses nickered neighs, while the chickens clucked diffidently. Raoul's subdued yet displeased crowing was ever present. Frankie reasoned that her presence was upsetting them but she didn't care.

She took a deep breath and tried to calm her nerves.

After leaving the Thatcher Ranch, she hadn't wanted to be around people, especially Adelaide or Uncle Elmer and their stated or implicit questions. She wanted to be alone and the barn was the only place she could think to do that. She needed to work it all out in her head, the before and after.

It's understandable, she told herself but the thought fell flat with a flash of a memory, horrible and new. Logan's face, slack, his eyes, lifeless.

The way he had looked at her—at all of them.

It was like he wasn't seeing her, wasn't seeing any of it. Anything that was Logan was dead and gone and Frankie had no idea if it was coming back.

Frankie swallowed.

He's coping, disengaging, she told herself but the thought did little to strike the way he'd looked at her from her mind. There had been no recognition, no emotion at all, like she was a wall or a fruit fly.

She wondered if that meant he blamed her, not that she could fault him if he did.

Frankie paused, realizing she'd been turning and turning the pendant in her hand. She let it drop from her hands, straightened her spine.

There was no point in jumping to dire conclusions now. The best thing she could do was act like a regular human being, and not go cloistering herself away in a dark barn, muttering to herself like a crazy person and disturbing the animals.

Knock-knock-na-knock-knock

"Frankie, you in here?"

She ground her teeth.

Who was I fooling thinking I could get a minute of peace?

For a moment, Frankie considered pretending she wasn't but she knew her sister wasn't going to leave her alone that easily.

"Yeah," she sighed.

"Good." The door creaked open, showing Adelaide's thin form. "Now stop sulking and come play 7-Up with me and Uncle Elmer."

Frankie didn't move.

"I don't know if I feel like it."

"Fran–"

"I know you don't get it, it's just..." Frankie's fists balled as she lashed out, all the emotion inside her spilling forth in a torrent. She couldn't even completely explain it herself, how Logan's reaction had cut into her on such a visceral level. "Addy, how he looked at me…"

"Don't blame yourself." Adelaide spoke with a sureness Frankie craved. "Anyway, I talked to Garrett, and there's more going on there than meets the eye."

Frankie met her sister's look evenly.

"What do you mean?"

"Logan's been through a lot, even before all this. Apparently, he saw something happen way, way back. Kind of messed him up. So, if this has got him acting all off, don't take it personally."

Frankie's brow furrowed with concern.

"What happened?" she asked, her heart growing heavy.

"I don't know the details," Addy said quickly and Frankie wondered if she was lying but she also knew her sister was like a locked vault when she wanted to be. "I just wanted to tell you that this doesn't have anything to do with you."

Frankie rolled her eyes at the innocence of her sister's statement.

"Logan just looked at me as if I were a ghost. How am I supposed to not take it personally?"

Adelaide sighed loudly.

"Fine. Take it personally, but would you please play 7-Up with Uncle Elmer and me?"

Frankie got up, glaring at her sister even though the dark meant she probably wouldn't see it.

"No," she snapped. "Close the door behind you."

She still wanted to be left alone.

CHAPTER 17

Logan

The next few weeks felt like the very same day over and over for Logan.

Mornings when he couldn't stop himself from checking his phone, there'd be a new missed call from Frankie, a new text. Angry or sad, resigned or hopeful, depending on the day.

- **Hey! Just thought I'd check in.**
- **Hey, are you still ignoring me?**
- **Hey, you won't believe what Gus just did!**
- **Are you really not going to respond?**
- **Are you okay? Garrett says you're not...**

Every message went unanswered but each one remained stored in the back of his mind for Logan to overthink later.

His brothers popped into his bedroom, with food he

barely ate and advice he didn't want. They badgered him to do his exercises, ones he did only to make them leave.

His physical therapy was a pointless exercise in pain. He'd learned that the first few times. He wasn't weak; he was boneless. This was how he was now, who he was. reminding him.

I'm an invalid.

The wheelchair wasn't as bad as he'd expected. It meant that no one expected him to go down the stairs, and he didn't. Logan spent a lot of time sitting around, not even thinking. His mind was fully committed to the haze. His days were a blur.

At one point, his brothers hauled the old VCR and Pa's old TV upstairs and put on some climbing videos. Logan pretended to watch until they left, only to turn them off as soon as his brothers disappeared.

They didn't understand. That was his old life. Watching the shows made him feel even more inadequate.

One day, Garrett came and wouldn't leave, even when Logan ignored him. Garrett's freckled face screwed into a scowl, his blue eyes narrowed.

"You can't keep doing this," Garrett told him.

Logan regarded him impassively without responding.

"I mean it." Garrett raked a hand through his hair. "You're not doing your physical therapy, you won't see Frankie, you just… sit there."

Logan continued to stare at him.

"Feeling sorry for yourself won't do you any good. Honestly, Logan, I know it sucks – losing climbing for this long, but if you just did your exercises..."

Logan turned away.

Garrett let out a low breath.

"We're at the end of our rope, Chase, Chance and me. We're thinking of telling Ma what happened, asking her to come back. She's asked about you a few times, wants to see you on Skype."

Logan found the word, even if he wasn't entirely sure of the reason for it.

"No."

Garrett strode over so he was in front of Logan's line of sight again.

"Then *do* something—do your physical therapy. Don't just sit here like your life is over."

Logan wasn't sure what to say to that.

"Logan?" Garrett crouched down. "I'm not making empty threats—you keep this up, and I'm calling Ma back home."

"Don't." Logan's body tensed to a coil. The last thing he wanted was for his mother to cut her trip short on his account.

"Then stop just sitting there. Stop giving up."

"I don't really have a choice in that, in case you haven't noticed."

"That's not what I meant. I just want you to do the exercises. Get out of the house a bit."

"I don't want to."

"Well, maybe it's not just up to you. Your brothers miss you, Frankie misses you."

"No."

They didn't miss him. The missed the man he'd been okay at pretending to be, for a while. This shell, this invalid was more fitting of who he was.

They're just seeing the real me now.

Logan scowled. The darkness, the hopelessness of his own thoughts annoyed him, disturbed him. But there was no way to get out of it, to change it. Before, he could climb—be free of it all. Now, there was nothing.

Even Frankie… something twisted in Logan at the thought of her.

No.

The last thing he needed was to see her looking at him how she'd looked at him last time. He couldn't bear to see the puzzlement and concern in her eyes. He couldn't take disappointing her a second time.

"One week." Garrett walked to the door. "I'll give you one more week to figure this out, start doing something. After that, I'm calling Ma."

Logan stared at the door and wondered what he would do in a week.

CHAPTER 18

Frankie

Two weeks.

Frankie lobbed her argyle sock at the wall, watching it fall in a pink swish with mild interest.

How had it been two weeks since she'd seen Logan? Two weeks of barn mucking and animal feeding with Uncle Elmer. Two weeks of enduring Adelaide's subtle and not-so-subtle hints that she should 'move on' and invite Andrew to Sagebrush? She could barely stomach the sight of Addy and Garrett smiling and walking hand and hand as if their happiness reminded her of everything she'd lost.

She reasoned that she had found some solace in Gus, who was getting fat and playful and she'd found a strawberry patch at the edge of Uncle Elmer's property that she went to sometimes when she wanted to be really, truly alone.

That wasn't what she wanted, of course. The one thing she really wanted was the one thing she couldn't have.

Logan.

Frankie rolled onto her side and stared into the wall.

She couldn't understand how the resilient, fun man she'd begun to fall for had turned into the shell of a man who wouldn't even respond her her texts.

Frankie couldn't take another one of those visits, the door-knocking, the waiting, the brothers' poorly disguised knowing and pitying looks. It's like they were wondering when she'd finally get the hint and let Logan go.

Every time she hauled herself all the way to Thatcher Ranch, Logan was "sleeping" and wouldn't see her.

Every single fricking time. Yeah right.

She'd seriously considered just marching up there and telling him off a few times, only she was scared of what she'd find at the top of those stairs.

"Yoo-hoo Frankie!" Adelaide called in.

"Go away," Frankie groaned. "I'm sleeping."

"It's 6 pm!" Uncle Elmer yelled. "You ain't foolin' nobody! Now get your lazy behind down this instant, you got a guest!"

Her head popped up, her heart jumping into her throat.

I knew he'd come around! I knew it!

All the anger and upset she'd been harvesting suddenly dissipated as she flew out of the room and down the stairs, a broad smile coloring her face. He was back, finally and—

She stopped in dead in her tracks when she saw who was standing in the entranceway of the farmhouse. It wasn't Logan.

It was Andrew.

CHAPTER 19

Logan

Dinner was late which was odd in itself.

Hunger kept Logan awake, striking clarity into things that normally weren't so obvious. A tree branch scraped against the window, the air was stuffy and scuzzy, something smelled rank in an undefinable way.

"Hello?" he called out to the house. "I'm starved!"

There was no response to his call and Logan strained his ears for signs of life below. Grumbling slightly, he pulled himself into the wheelchair and wheeled over to the door, poking his head out.

"Hello?" he tried again.

He didn't yell very loud. Raising his voice would take too much effort, and he was already exhausted as it was. Those days, he was always exhausted. As he furthered his way out onto the landing, he wondered where those walkie-talkies were that his brothers always stuck to him when he was climbing.

He could hear his family downstairs, voices low. Logan knew if he wheeled over to the top of the stairs, then called again, they'd probably hear him. Sighing, he continued over the hallway but before he could open his mouth to get their attention, he heard a word that made his pause.

"...Frankie."

Logan stopped and listened.

"Should we tell him?" Chase asked.

"I don't know." Garrett's voice was uneasy. "It might make him worse."

"Or smarten up," Chance said caustically. "Once he hears his girl is moving on—"

"She isn't moving on," Garrett snapped. "Not yet. Her ex came back on his own accord."

"Still," Chase argued. "With Logan giving her the cold shoulder and her old guy back, she's not likely to hold out forever."

"I'm surprised she's kept at it for as long as she has," Garrett admitted. "She must really care about him."

A peculiar feeling overcame Logan then and he slowly wheeled back to his room, closing the door behind him.

He'd heard enough.

His first instinct was to clamber into bed and let sleep overtake him. That was what he always did when matters got too heavy but this time, something was jabbing at him, something hard and clear.

I'm losing her...

Logan shook his head angrily.

You never had her, you idiot.

Images were twisting into him, harder and harder, the memories had to escape now that the floodgates had opened.

Red-red swirls of hair, eyes that stole the sky's blue. Lips curled with a smile or something that could be any number of things.

His hands clasping the necklace around her neck.

Her words, quiet and awed and grateful, her eyes even more with her head tipped to his: "This. Thank you."

Frankie. *Frankie Mills.*

Logan clenched his hand into a fist, then watched it unclench.

Haven't I lost enough already? I have to lose Frankie too?

But he didn't have the energy to fight. She deserved better than a weak, broken man.

She deserves a man like her ex...

It was impossible to hear the voice in his head reminding him that she had chosen him, not Andrew.

Logan sat up straighter, then slumped in his seat.

But maybe, if you went there...

The thought rolled and unrolled, rolled and unrolled. Until something disturbed it.

A knock broke through him, a voice shattering his semi-haze.

"Hey, it's Chance. You awake?"

The door opened and Logan stared at the unwelcome and unexpected guest. Out of all the brothers, Chance had come the least but that wasn't surprising to Logan. It was surprising to see him there in that moment, an almost sheepish expression on his face.

"Hi," Logan said flatly. He didn't add, "what do you want?" as he was sure his expression implied. Chance didn't look at him, his eyes wandering around the room as if there was anything other than the walls that Logan had stripped bare since the accident.

"Listen, the others don't want to tell you, but there's something you should know."

"I head," Logan said flatly. Chance glanced to him, slightly shocked.

"Oh, right. Well." Chance put his hands on his bone spur belt buckle. "I wasn't going to tell you to be a jerk. I just figured, if it were me, I'd want to know."

"Okay."

Logan wasn't sure what to think. Messing around with him was Chance's usual M.O., but then again, since the accident, Chance hadn't been acting like his usual self at all. Logan idly considered that his brother felt shame about how everything had transpired.

When Chance looked at him again, his brother's blue eyes were curved with defiance.

"And I know you've always thought I was a jerk to you, and thing is, I just wanted to say that..." His mouth screwed up, as though an external force were forcing the words out, then he exhaled, gave a jerky nod. "You're right."

His gaze lowered, and he kicked at something on the floor that wasn't there. Logan's eyebrows raised with slight skepticism but he didn't speak as Chance went on.

"All the time we were growing up, I hated how... well, *weird*, you were. Like it was a reminder of how messed up our family was. Giving away the whole thing to others. I didn't get why you couldn't just pretend better like the rest of us."

Chance's mouth twisted.

"And then I found out what happened, what you found, and I understood a bit better, but I still hated it."

Logan could only stare at him. Even if he were given days to think of a decent response, he knew he'd come up with clean nothing. This was the last thing he'd expected from Chance.

"But this accident," Chance's voice broke, "made me realize that I've been punishing you for what happened with Pa. Blaming you. But that wasn't your fault. This accident—goading you into getting on the back of that horse —was my fault. And I'm sorry."

There were some words. Logan could feel them inside his

chest, brimming and surging and bubbling and forming like new hot coals.

"You don't have to say anything." Chance was already making for the door. "I didn't come here for your forgiveness. Just something I thought you should know."

He paused and gave Logan a hard look.

"Listen, I get it. After how Ma and Pa ended up…" He shook his head. "Let's just say I don't see myself settling down with anyone anytime soon."

An exhale followed his words.

"But you don't have to make the same mistakes. And that Frankie of yours, well…you get a woman like that, I'd say you'd be a dang idiot to let her slip away."

His brother turned to scurry away but Logan's voice rang out, surely and clear.

"Will you help me downstairs?"

Chance paused and gave his brother a glance before a small nod of approval and smirk filled his face.

"Dang right I will. It's high time you finally saw the light, Logey."

In minutes, Logan was outside the ranch, leaning back on his wheelchair and staring out at the open fields. Chance lingering tentatively behind as Logan inhaled the sweet-smelling country air.

"Do you want some help?" Chance asked when Logan didn't move. The younger brother shook his head.

"No," Logan firmly. "I need to do this myself."

CHAPTER 20

Frankie

Frankie opened her dresser drawer to glare at the blue stone necklace, her fingers quivering above the piece before slamming the drawer shut again.

When are you going to stop with this? You need to let it go.

She reasoned that she wasn't wearing the stone all the time now but she had it stashed where she could look at it with more frequency than she should have. Even if it was to open the drawer and shoot it a glare, like it was a conduit to the ire she was feeling toward Logan.

Sighing, Frankie turned to peer out the window. One storey down, Andrew crouched beside Uncle Elmer, helping him fix his perpetually dying and resurrecting car. She looked away quickly.

He doesn't even know what the heck he's doing. He's only pretending to impress Uncle Elmer, Frankie thought with a scowl on her face. She didn't remind herself that at least Andrew had shown up, that he was there when Logan wasn't.

"Are you going to hide in your room all day?" Adelaide

asked from outside the door in an annoyingly patronizing tone.

"Are you going to hound me for the rest of our lives?" Frankie shot back.

Adelaide creaked the door open a crack so Frankie could see that she was wearing a condescending smile to match her tone.

"Maybe. I am your sister after all."

"Believe it or not, some sisters are friends. Allies."

Addy's expression turned haughty.

"And as your ally, I'm here to tell you that you're being an idiot about Andrew."

"I didn't ask him here."

"Which further proves my point."

Frankie sighed loudly.

"Honestly, things are over with Andrew. I appreciate him coming here, I really do. But I just don't feel that way about him."

Adelaide flounced inside, her chiffon skirt swishing around her legs as her hands went to her hips.

"Just tell me one thing. Would your beloved Logan have come all this way *after you'd broken up with him* just to see if you'd give him another chance? Would he be down there with Uncle Elmer, helping him fix some beat-up 67' pickup that has no business being fixed for the, like, fifteenth time?"

Frankie's gaze was locked on the window, on the two figures outside, working away.

"Sorry that I can't assign my feelings at will to whichever guy likes me best, Addy."

Adelaide's voice was quiet, sorry.

"Well, maybe you should. Maybe you should start thinking about being with the kind of guy who treats you best."

Frankie turned to her with an angry response on her lips, a quick comeback, but it died away.

Her sister was right and denying it would only make her the liar in this scenario.

Wasn't I just thinking the same thing myself?

Addy was annoying, patronizing, meddling, and, most incongruously of all, right.

It twisted inside Frankie like a small knife to the heart.

She was sitting there pining over some guy who couldn't be bothered to even respond to one of her many texts and calls.

He didn't even have the decency to give me some closure so I wouldn't sit around, worried about him.

Frankie settled back on her bed, indignation and upset rocking her gut.

"Go away."

Her tone was flat, low; her heart wasn't in it.

Adelaide stepped forward, her face and tone softening,

"Hey, listen, I'm sorry, okay?"

Frankie turned to face the wall.

"Just go away. Please."

She didn't have the energy for more squabbling. She just needed to be alone.

"Frankie..."

"Go away."

Finally, Addy obliged, perhaps hearing just how broken her sister really was.

∼

The sweet waft of buttery corn aroused Frankie from an unsettling on-and-off nap, one she hadn't realized she'd fallen into.

"Dinner?" she called, already clambering out of bed.

"Hold your horses, it's comin' in another hour or so!" Uncle Elmer yelled from somewhere in the house. "

Ignoring his timeline, she raced to the kitchen. She was so intent on hurrying and mentally salivating over corn that she almost ran clean into Andrew.

I keep forgetting he's here.

"Sorry." She backed away, staring at him as if he were a stranger. She'd forgotten how wide-set and kind his brown eyes were, and was reminded of how tall he was.

"Ha, it's fine." He tried to smile, but he looked at her all sad, like he'd lost her again.

God, I've been a fool. He's a perfectly good man standing right in front of me. Why can't I love him?

"I'm sorry," she blurted out.

A smile quirked in one lip corner.

"You already said that."

"I know, I—"

Suddenly, Frankie felt entombed in this too warm and too crowded house. Her gaze snuck to the door, then back to Andrew.

"Walk with me?" she asked. Andrew's face lit up at her suggestion and he nodded.

"Sounds like a plan." Andrew smiled, and something moved in Frankie. "Haven't got to see the full extent of your uncle's farm. You can show me the lay of the land."

They headed outside and Frankie paused to take a deep breath.. She paused to take a deep breath. She could feel Andrew peering at her, even if her gaze was on the sky, fixed on a rhino shaped cloud.

"You okay?" he asked, sensing her disconsolation.

"Not really," she confessed, "I…"

She let the words trail off. As much as she liked to be open, discussing the Logan issue with Andrew would have been cruel.

"How's Richmond?" she asked instead.

"Ah, you know. It's Richmond." He shrugged, dipped his head from side to side. "Penny Lane is still a good Saturday night. Cops are still actually arresting people for jaywalking. Everyone misses you."

Frankie smiled. It was nice to know, as different as things were here, that back home everything was the same, just waiting for her to return.

Her smile wavered almost as soon as it formed.

Hadn't that been her whole reason for leaving Richmond in the first place? Hadn't life become stagnant there?

A lot of good a change did you, she thought caustically. Her feet began to move before she realized it and Andrew hurried to keep up as she'd known he would.

"I'm sorry about how I left," Frankie muttered, not meeting his eyes. "I just... I'm not good at goodbyes and I didn't know what to say."

Andrew nodded, taking that in step.

"It was hard at first, I won't say it wasn't. I didn't understand it." He took a good look around. "But I can see now why you'd want to come here."

Frankie glanced his way.

"Oh yeah?"

His nod was sure.

"Yeah. All the fresh air and space, the animals. The calm. It's a good place to think."

"You'd think, wouldn't you?" Frankie murmured, too quiet for him to hear. Any thinking she'd done had only twisted he up inside.

"I heard about what you did for that stray cat too," Andrew was saying now. "That was real nice of you."

"You would've done the same." Frankie smiled at the thought. It was true. "Gus was all skin and bones, but now he's... he's pretty okay. Or getting there at least."

Andrew's lip corners turned up teasing.

"You gonna introduce me?"

"Ha, guess we'll have to see." Frankie bit her lip. Joking with Andrew was easy. Being with him was easy, certainly easier than it had ever been with Logan.

"Maybe you should start thinking about being with the kind of guy who treats you best."

Had she escaped her old life, tried to find a new one, just to find that it was the old one that was right for her all along?

At least Andrew had never broken her heart.

"We'd better go back." Frankie turned to face the speck that was the farm. "Uncle Elmer and his corn waits for no man."

She found herself staring at the property for a long moment. She realized that Andrew was right. The ranch here was a good place to think.

As soon as dinner was done, Frankie intended to do just that—alone and uninterrupted, possibly for the first time since arriving.

~

Dinner with Uncle Elmer, Andrew and Adelaide went well. They upheld an easy chit-chat, Andrew skillfully leading Uncle Elmer away from a full account of every truck repair he'd ever made. Still, Frankie was happy to be alone in her room after it was all said and done.

She couldn't shake the image of Logan's lifeless face back at his house, and his words… "Do you want me to leave?"

She didn't grab a book, or watch a video on her phone to distract from it. Instead, she took the hilt of the knife in her heart – *he doesn't care, things are over* – and twisted it deeper.

She looked at the glaring line of her unanswered messages and calls, one by one. Read the messages.

- **Hey, I know we left things weird last time, but I thought that maybe…**
- **You can't ignore me forever… Seriously Logan…**
- **Hello?...**
- **I actually have something important to tell you…**

She counted out the days since she'd last heard from him.
Twenty-two. Twenty-two days of unanswered texts. I think it's safe to say that he's done with me too.

Frankie dropped the phone on her nightstand and got up.

Uncle Elmer sat on the back porch, smoking his pipe and Adelaide was off with Garrett. Andrew in the guest room, calling home and Frankie was able to leave without anyone noticing.

Even outside, the night was busy without her. An owl hooted, the stars hung brighter than normal and the air carried a heavy dampness.

As she walked, Frankie let her hands hang free, catch on the taller grasses; Buffalo, Bermuda, St. Augustine.

This was it.

Her body was hyper-alive with excitement and fear and an early resignation. Even as some small part of her hoped otherwise, she knew what she was going to find at Thatcher Ranch.

Frankie took in a shape in the corner of her eye moving towards her, but she didn't make the connection, until she swung around and stopped.

He moved jaggedly, like a drunken scarecrow, and she would've laughed, thought it was a joke, if she didn't recognize the blond hair.

Am I imagining this?

But as she blinked, she realized that her eyes weren't

deceiving her. It was him. After three weeks, she was staring at Logan Thatcher.

"Logan?"

Even though he was sitting and she was standing, he looked at her full in the face. In that one look, in those curved hazel eyes, she saw everything.

His pain and regret and guilt.

His want and hope and need for a second chance with her, to get back what they had, what he'd never had before.

Somehow, the space and distance between them was filled and her face met his. Finally, blissfully, Logan kissed her.

CHAPTER 21

Logan

The world around them quieted to a near fade.

The feel of her lips was…

There was no comparison, not by any stretch of the imagination.

It was better than his mother's apple cinnamon pancakes, better than a breathless laugh on a summer day, better than the highest, hardest summit he'd ever peaked.

It was Frankie Mills, the feeling of possibility, and a thrumming that took him over inside out.

The last of the haze neutralized, shattered into a thousand tiny pieces of clarity and suddenly, Logan was there again, entirely and wholly.

Frankie peeled away for breath, and they stayed there, foreheads tipped together.

The words came then in a torrent, ones he'd been holding onto for far too long.

"I've been an idiot. A fool. I didn't want you to see me as

weak, so I stayed away. Then the longer it went, the harder it got. I didn't know what to say to you. I've never thought I was good enough for you."

Frankie opened her mouth to say something, but Logan quieted her with his fingers on her lips.

"Wait. I need to say this. Say it all before I lose the nerve." He swallowed. "Ever since I was little, I never thought good things could happen to me. I figured I didn't deserve it."

His breath caught.

"When I was a kid, I caught my Pa yelling at Ma, punching the wall, throwing every pot and pan we had at the wall. The others were at our aunt's place, and I had had to stay home because I had the flu. That night, I hid around the corner and watched and did nothing. Just shut down. And got so mad that I wanted to hurt him, my Pa, smash him into the wall. It scared me and made me sure I was like him. And I didn't tell the others after that. I kept to myself, sure they'd find out. Pa got worse as the years went on, and soon we all knew what he was."

There was a silence, where all the shards settled into place. Frankie wrapped her arms around him.

"My God. Logan, I'm so sorry, I'm…" Her hand stroked along his head. "I had no idea. I…"

She turned away to shake her head, a thousand different expressions crossing her face. She heaved a sigh, her shoulders following the movement.

When she turned back to face him, he instantly recognized the look she gave him, although he didn't know it well.

"Logan. You are the gentlest man I've ever known."

Loved. She means loved.

The air was sweet with the feeling. The moon itself was a jaunty smile.

She knew him. She saw him like no one ever had before.

Every part of him, even the worst, darkest parts he'd kept stashed away for as long as he could remember.

Her eyes held a crinkle of laughter when she pulled back to look at him.

"But if you think that's going to scare me off, you've got another thing coming. Your family doesn't have a copyright on being messed up. Mine never wanted me. I was an accident, and my mom almost gave me up for adoption."

As her face contorted with emotion, Logan reached to hold her, to make it better.

"I wasn't supposed to find out, but during some dumb family feud, my cousin and I got drunk together, and it came out. My cousin told me how my Mom got hit by postpartum depression hard. How she and my Dad separated for almost a year. How she couldn't take looking after me."

Frankie's gaze was on her feet.

"Still, it makes a small part of me feel unworthy. She had no problems loving Addy, you know? But with me, it was different."

"I'm sorry." She moved closer, so Logan could squeeze her tight and he held her against him protectively.

"I am too." But Frankie was beaming, squeezing him just as tightly. "Because now, you are *never* getting rid of me."

As they sank into each other once again, more words sprang out of Logan before he could grab them and put them in line.

"That's the idea."

Logan didn't know how long they'd been in the hug, only that his body reacted when Frankie pulled away.

"Okay, first things first – your exercises."

Logan groaned, unhappy to break the spell between them. Frankie planted her feet firmly in the ground.

"Yes, Mr. Thatcher, and I won't have any argument. If you

want to be with me, then you'll have to do them. Simple as that."

"Even if—"

"Yes."

"And what about—"

"*Yes.*"

Logan exhaled, but he was smiling.

"All right, I guess I'll do them then."

He moved to hold her again, but Frankie stepped back, wagging a finger in his face.

"Uh-uh. You are not getting out of it that easy."

"I can't exactly do them now," Logan protested.

"Why not?" Frankie made a show of peering around the ground, then the sky. "Are there secret rattlesnakes all around here I don't know about? Is a torrential hurricane on its way?"

"Maybe." Logan grinned.

My girl sure is something.

"Fine, but even if I wanted to, I don't have the exercises memorized by heart."

"Not a problem." Frankie smiled evilly as she wagged her phone. "I happen to have several videos downloaded on my phone."

Logan had to chuckle.

"There really is no way out of this, is there?"

"Not on my watch."

As Frankie's phone chorused, "All You Need is Love" on a loop, and the videos coached Logan through straight leg raises, ankle inversions and eversions, Logan came to believe the lyrics.

Trite as it was, the song title had it right.

With Frankie by his side, with love in his heart, anything was possible.

All he had needed was love.

CHAPTER 22

Frankie

The rest was history to Frankie's mind.

She was stunned that Logan wheeled his way to Uncle Elmer and Adelaide and apologized for how he'd behaved. He'd endured their badgering, and card game playing (and Uncle Elmer's ludicrous cheating), and cross-examining day after day, until even they were sufficiently convinced that he wasn't going anywhere—not this time.

It filled Frankie with some guilt the way Andrew had left but true to his Southern charm, her ex had shaken Logan's hand on his way out, some regret in his eyes.

"I hope you're worthy of her," was the only parting shot that Andrew could muster but Logan's response had warmed her heart.

"One day, I hope to be."

Frankie loved how Logan and his brothers and her and Addy started having meals together regularly. The family suppers grew into feasts and later, movie nights. There were

Westerns for the twins, thrillers for Garrett, documentaries for Logan, and comedies for her and Adelaide.

She and Logan whiled away whole afternoons watching the goats. Potens, Fortem and Forti played with Gus waving sage grass in his face and tossing rubber balls for him to chance. The little guy was cute and funny, causing them to laugh until Uncle Elmer would stop by, muttering about idleness being a shortcut to death.

Logan started doing his exercises with a doggedness bordering on obsession, even without her supervision. The more time he spent with Frankie, the wider his smiles became. As a result of his unwavering efforts, he quickly moved from the wheelchair to crutches, and then, finally, limping in what felt like record time.

One night, on a Skype call with her parents, Frankie explained why she was choosing to stay in Sagebrush another few months. Logan introduced himself to her parents via video chat. Frankie wasn't sure how her parents felt about him, not through that medium but she realized she didn't care either. She was happy and sure of what she wanted.

The next day, on his own Skype call, Logan introduced her to a woman with his same eyes and a knit Incan poncho —his Ma. Unlike her parents' lukewarm response to Logan, Cora Thatcher seemed delighted to cyber meet Frankie and her approval only furthered the feeling that all was right to Frankie.

One day, Frankie asked him, "Do you think it's time?"

She'd been tentatively turning it around in her mind for weeks, ever since Logan had ditched the crutches.

Is he better enough? Would climbing be too risky?

The last thing she wanted to do was for Logan to get hurt again, especially at her suggestion. The shame she felt from what had happened in town hadn't entirely dissipated, even though she knew Logan didn't blame her. Yet she saw how his gaze often wandered to the far-off slope of the mountain, and she knew what he needed to feel as complete as she did. Logan needed climbing like otters need water.

Logan's face was guarded, but she could still spot the excitement brimming there.

"You think I am?" he asked uncertainly but Frankie knew he was only waiting for absolution on what he'd already decided for himself.

"I don't know," she confessed. "It's just something Adelaide and I were talking about the other day. We thought it might be a nice day trip for the group, if nothing else. And you know how I like day trips."

Logan smiled.

"Oh, do I ever."

In fact, ever since he'd found out, Logan had planned several little outings. There had been a trip to a secluded lily-pad filled pond, some hipster comedy at the local theater, a gallery tour of a neighboring artsy small town. Each excursion had shown Logan to be stronger and more confident.

"Is that a yes?" Frankie pressed, then shot him a warning glare. "Though I don't want you to push it. At all."

"We can go and I can try and see." Logan shrugged, smiled. "Doesn't hurt to try."

Frankie smiled too.

"I'll tell the others, see what they think. Tomorrow?"

Logan nodded.

"Tomorrow."

Twenty-four hours later, the ancient Thatcher pickup puttered along the backroads.

The twins took turns complaining about Garrett's driving, then chucking recently roasted almonds at unwary passersby.

"How are you related to them?" Adelaide asked Garrett who grinned in his nonchalant way.

"Pretty sure they were adopted," he replied. The response earned him a roasted almond to the skull.

Logan held Frankie's hand while the fingers of her free hand tapped a nervous beat into her lap.

Am I making a mistake? Another one?

Logan had promised to be cautious, but what if he made it up a certain amount, then his legs failed him?

She forced her tapping hand still.

The twins and Garrett can help him. That's why were doing things this way.

She snuck a glance at Logan's face but his expression was placid, giving away nothing.

"Logan?"

"Yeah?"

"Do you think… are you sure…"

He squeezed her hand.

"Yeah. It's going to be fine."

She wished she shared his confidence.

In the front seats, Adelaide and Garrett were having a similar conversation.

"I just don't think… for your first time," Garrett began.

"That I should even go up one measly rock?" Adelaide demanded. "What am I, a china doll? I won't break if I fall, and I won't even fall anyway. That's what the climbing thingy is for."

"You don't even know what it's called," Garrett sighed.

"Neither do you!"

"Maybe not, but I've climbed a handful of times before. I just think, to play it safe…"

"How am I supposed to ever learn if I don't try? Plus, Frankie's going."

"She's already gone."

"*Garrett.*" Frankie knew what that tone meant. "I'm going. And that's final."

In the back, Chance whistled long. "These Mills women mean business."

Frankie smirked at him.

"And don't you forget it."

"Anyway, we're here," Chase pointed out as Garrett pulled into the parking lot.

Last chance to stop this.

Frankie clasped Logan's hand tightly.

"You ready?" His smile was teasing.

"I guess, just… you be careful!"

He brushed a curl out of her face.

"Dang, you're more nervous about this than when you went the first time."

"Yeah, well, last time…"

He took her hand, pressed it to his kiss.

"It's going to be fine."

Frankie repeated the same words to herself as they began to set up. The twins went up first to set up the top rope anchor and ropes. Chance paused to call down to Logan.

"Still don't get why you prefer this to rodeo!"

Logan grinned back at his brother.

"Still don't get why you prefer rodeo to this!"

Frankie smiled too, realizing that the animus that had existed between them once seemed to have evaporated.

The mountain loomed overhead. It was stepper and taller than Frankie remembered. There was no wind, not even much sound, as if nature itself was holding its breath for what was to come.

Logan wrapped his strong arms around her, held her tight.

"You ready?"

Frankie tried to smile.

"Will you not go if I say no?"

Logan kissed her ear.

"It's going to be all right."

Frankie heaved a breath, letting herself sink fully into his arms.

Then she straightened herself.

You heard the man.

"I'll go first," Logan said, already attaching himself to the rope.

Which was just fine with Frankie. If he started to fall—

Frankie gave her head a shake.

He's not going to fall.

"It's okay, Frankie," Logan called back, already moving up the mountain a few feet. He waved an arm. "See?"

Frankie eyed him warily, her heart in her throat.

"I mean it. If you so much as feel an odd twinge–"

But Logan had already moved on and Frankie could only watch with a begrudging awe.

That's my man.

Logan melded into the rock like he belonged there, an animal returning to its natural habitat.

He paused to toss an expectant look back at her.

"You coming or not?"

Frankie just grinned.

"All right then. Hold your horses."

Hold your horses? Uncle Elmer is rubbing off on me.

Strangely, the realization didn't bother her as much as it might have months ago. Perhaps it was the headiness of the day, watching Logan as he climbed in his element. She took hold and moved up one rock.

A low exclamation made her freeze. Her head instantly jerked up and she saw Logan. He was on a ledge, breathing unevenly on all fours.

Her stomach dropped. His face was clenched with pain.

"Logan!"

His head bowed in a sort of nod, his jaw working.

"I know."

She paused, gave him time for it even though it was going against every instinct inside her.

He exhaled.

"I'm coming down."

But he didn't move.

"You need help?" Garrett called from above.

"I'm good." Logan's voice was steady, but that didn't mean anything. "Just give me a minute."

"Are you sure?" Frankie said with panic in her voice.

"Don't make this harder than it already is." His voice was curt. Frankie scrambled back to the ground, her eyes fixed on Logan. Everything felt heavy, constricting.

This was her fault. This was her idea, and now he was disappointed, if not hurt. Logan slowly began his descent and Frankie forced herself to keep quiet. He moved with a tense gradualness that she hoped wasn't disguising an injury.

Little by little, he picked his way down. At some points, he stopped so long that Frankie was sure she should say something, offer help, or even just say something encouraging or funny but the words stuck in her mouth like honey.

He needs to focus. Leave him be.

Only once he had both feet flat on the ground, did Frankie release a breath she hadn't even realized she was holding.

He's okay.

Logan kept his eyes down, and Frankie almost feared to look him in the face, at what she'd find there. Instead, she patted his arm, forced her voice into a normal tone.

"There. That wasn't so bad, was it?"

A too-long pause and Frankie's gut lurched.

No, I won't lose him again, I–

"Guess not." Logan tried to smile, but couldn't manage to tug his mouth up into it. Even so, she was relieved he was speaking and not looking through her like she wasn't there.

Frankie plopped on the ground.

"Let's just sit here and eat the Oreos I brought. Let the others climb to their hearts' content."

Logan sat down, his breaths still labored. He waved Frankie away.

"Thanks, babe. But I want you to go."

Frankie scowled. "I want to stay and feed you Oreos."

Logan shook his head.

"Not getting to see you climb would be a double disappointment. Please."

His eyes said the rest.

Being a burden would be worse.

Frankie sighed, pausing after she rose to see if he'd change his mind. But also she saw was an encroaching smile.

"Fine."

"He just wants to look at your butt!" Chance called down from above.

They howled, as Logan fully smiled.

"Got me," he confessed.

"Any chance you'd mind throwing up a couple of Oreos?" Chase wondered. "Climbing makes the belly grow lighter."

Garrett snorted.

"You've been climbing for six minutes."

"Yeah, and we're only asking for two Oreos," Chance argued. "Each."

But Frankie had already started to climb, leaving the cookies with Logan.

"Sorry boys. They'll be our victory present."

Suddenly, she felt like she was rushing. She knew that Logan had put on a brave face despite his disappointment.

THE COWBOY'S ONE AND ONLY

The best thing to do was just get this over with so she could return to him.

"Whoa superwoman," Adelaide said, as Frankie sped-climbed past her.

Frankie didn't pause, although she did smirk at her sister.

"What can I say? I learned from the best."

She was fast to pass the twins two, since they were more interested in eating the M and M's that someone had scrounged up.

"I can see the Oreo need was dire," she commented as she passed, although she did accept one proffered blue M and M before continuing on.

As she ascended, so too did the heavy feeling in her gut. Even without Logan, climbing was exhilarating. She was once again reminded of just why he liked it.

The view was spectacular and the height was intoxicating. Not to mention the adrenaline pumping through her veins.

Frankie felt an odd tug but she ignored it, continuing forth.

"Hold it!" someone cried out sharply.

That was the last thing she heard before she fell.

The rope around her jolted, then snapped. Frantically, she grabbed for something, anything, her hands coming onto a ledge.

Her hold shaking, Frankie's gaze fell to the land far below, down to the jagged rocks which would break her body into pieces when she landed.

Her hands slipped against the stone.

Frankie knew she was about to die.

CHAPTER 23

Logan

"We'll get her," the twins yelled in unison.

Someone said something else, but Logan didn't hear them. He didn't see anything but Frankie dangling precariously on the ledge.

About to fall.

He couldn't let it happen. He wouldn't.

This haze was different. It was focused, driving. It was fixed on Frankie.

The rock felt familiar under his hands. His climbing gear wasn't on but Logan didn't notice. Cries met his ears but Logan could only hear Frankie's.

Hand over hand, he climbed, one hold to the next.

Rock to rock to rock.

He passed Adelaide.

Garrett.

The twins.

They all called out, reaching for him but he avoided their panicked attempts.

He reached Frankie just as her hand fell away. She was holding onto the rocky ledge with one slippering grip, the fear in her face almost palpable.

Their eyes met.

"Logan…" she whispered, her luminous eyes filled with tears.

"Grab my hand."

Crumbling started from somewhere. A crack appeared in the ledge he was on. It wasn't sturdy enough for both their weight but he couldn't move until he had her in his arms.

If he held on, they would both fall.

"Let me go," Frankie sobbed.

"I'm not letting go." More crackling followed his statement. "Grab my hand."

She lunged up and missed him, causing more shaking beneath them.

"LOGAN!" she howled.

"AGAIN!" he insisted.

Once more, she threw herself upward and this time, he was ready. She landed against him.

Logan yanked her up into his arms and dropped back as the hold beneath them gave way.

He held fast to her, feeling the race of her heart match his. They sat in still silence, struggling to regain their breath. Finally, Frankie dropped her head back to stare up at him.

"Thank… you."

Her face was white as she strained to look at him, her eyes surreal shade of blue. Her fingers skidded across his face. "My… hero."

"Your boyfriend," Logan corrected her with a kiss on her forehead. She said something else, but pain arced up and blurred the edges of Logan's vision.

There another crumbling sensation, but this one from inside his head.

Frankie's fingers skidding elsewhere.

Frankie's voice called out as other words flew at him in all directions but he was fading away again.

And then there was darkness.

∽

When Logan came to they were safely at the bottom of the formation. Frankie peered over him, the concern on her face etched with exasperation and affection.

"Are you insane?" She groaned, the furious shake of her head sending her red curls splaying wildly. "This is exactly what I didn't want to happen. Logan!"

"I had to do it," Logan said simply and without regret.

He caught her gaze, made her understand. There was no other option.

A life without Frankie was no life at all. He'd done that and he never wanted to experience it again.

She splatted down on the ground beside him, as the others packed up the gear.

"My boyfriend, huh?" Frankie said teasingly.

"That's me," Logan answered. The sun was too bright, he had to squint to see Frankie. "And as your boyfriend, I would like the honor of taking you out to ice cream."

Frankie giggled. He tipped his head to hers to offer her another sweet kiss.

Everything was going to be all right.

He knew that now.

EPILOGUE

Frankie, Two Months Later

"And now, ladies and gents, we have Chance Thatcher up to the bull. We just saw how well his twin brother Chase rode that bad boy. Let's see if this cowboy can top it!"

After the announcer's braying voice fell silent, the crowd exploded out a deafening cheer.

Frankie smirked. As with Chase, it was louder than all the other contestants, probably due to the twins' sizable base of female groupies.

She leaned in closer to Logan so his scent would win out over the others. The mingling aromas of animal and popcorn were making her feel a little nauseous.

As Chance strode out to more applause, Frankie snuck a look at Logan. His shoulders were two up-jut rounds of tension, his eyes far-off fixities.

Is he nervous about his brother?

She didn't think that was it but she also didn't have a clue what else it might be and it wasn't the time to ask.

As they watched Chance hold onto the bull for dear life as the bull bucked, the tension didn't ebb in Logan's body. Nor did it grow.

Frankie forced herself to watch all the way through, as Chance's face contorted with effort, as the crowd shrieked and crowed until, finally, he was thrown off.

There were only a few more contestants after him, thankfully. Going to a rodeo had been a fun, new adventure for Frankie but she now knew it wasn't her thing.

It took some time for Chance and Chase to detach themselves from their mob of distraught female admirers but when they finally managed, they found Frankie and Logan without effort.

Chance grinned impishly.

"Who wants to drown their sorrows in cheap chicken wings with me at Molly Bloom's?"

"We already had a reservation booked," Garrett reminded him.

"Ah, yes." Chance nodded sagely. "So, who wants to drown their sorrows in chicken wings with me at Molly Bloom's?"

"Well, with an invitation like that," Frankie looped her arm through Logan's, "how could we say no?"

"You had me at cheap chicken wings," Adelaide admitted.

The group chatted easily as they made their way to the cars, although Frankie's heart wasn't in it. Not when Logan was still off how he was.

When they arrived at Logan's newly-purchased used Honda, Logan had recently bought, they found themselves alone. Frankie glanced at Logan, but his gaze was already on the parking lot as he turned the key in the ignition.

"Is something bothering you?"

He kept his eyes ahead of him.

"I'm good."

"No, you're not."

"You're reading into things."

"Fine, whatever." Frankie turned to look out her window as Logan pulled out of the parking lot and onto the highway. The land near the rodeo was an ugly wasteland. "Just remember, I *will* bother you until you tell me."

"I'm willing to live with that, seeing as there's nothing wrong," Logan replied.

They drove to Molly Bloom's in silence, but for the low drone of old country music on the radio through the blast of air conditioner.

They regrouped with the others, their smiles strained, hoping that the others wouldn't notice their tension. Frankie knew that the last thing Logan wanted was his family prying into his problems, whatever they might be. It would only serve to shut him down more.

The others were in too jovial a mood to notice anything else. It was contagious, the twins cheering and high fiving each other when they found out they wouldn't have to wait for a table, Garrett and Adelaide playfully arguing with a back and forth, "No, you tell them!" "No, *you* tell them!"

By the time they got to their seats, just about beaming, Adelaide broke them the news.

"I'm sure you all know already, but I've decided to stay in Sagebrush for a while longer."

"Huh." Chance scratched his head. "Why's that?"

Chase elbowed Garrett, all smirky.

"Can't be this oaf here."

"Nah." Garrett smiled sweetly at the twins, using his hat to gesture to them. "It was both your losses today that inspired her pity so much she—*hey*!"

He grabbed the coaster that Chance had chucked and placed it carefully back on the table.

"Careful now. That coaster almost– okay, *now you're in for it!*"

He frisbeed the second coaster, sending it plonking into Chance's eyebrow.

Chance's hand jabbed up as his brows jumped in outrage.

"Ow!"

Something was tinkling and it took them a few seconds to calm down and realize what it was. Chase hit his water glass with a spoon.

"Can I just say something?"

"Sure," Garrett's placid tone matched his expression, "but Chance better know that if his hand so much as *inches* towards that dang coaster–"

"Jerkturd," Chance grumbled, although his hands stayed at his sides.

Chase lifted a cup.

"I just wanted to congratulate Logan."

Logan shifted in his seat and looked at his brother in surprise.

"Me?"

"Yeah, you." Chase turned so that he was facing his brother. "You've come a long way these past few months."

"But—"

"Eh, eh, eh, I have a few words to say on that subject too." Chance leapt upright and held up a hand to stop Logan from interrupted.

Garrett rolled his eyes.

"Why am I not surprised?"

"Despite my tragic loss today—"

"Thought this was supposed to be about Logan," Chase cut in, clearly peeved about being interrupted.

"Shut it, you." Chance drew himself up pompously. "As I was saying before I was *so rudely interrupted...* Logan, my boy, we haven't always seen eye to eye, and in the past I've been a bit of a—"

"Jerk," Garrett supplied helpfully.

"Pissant?" Chase provided.

Frankie giggled into her palm.

Chance ignored them.

"Point is, you cut a fine figure now. Running the ranch as well as any of us, earning money on the side training people rock climbing. Ma would be proud."

"Speaking of which," Garrett rose too, "I have some news too."

"Well, if we're all standing…" Chase shrugged as he got to his feet.

"Can one of you let the others speak without interrupting?" Adelaide asked with an exasperated sigh, staying firmly seated.

"Hear, hear," Frankie agreed.

"News is," Garrett continued blithely, "Ma's coming home."

"What! When?" Chance was so surprised he dropped the coaster he'd picked up at some point.

"Next week," Garrett said, glaring at him. "It was supposed to be a surprise, but then I heard you two planning your consolation Las Vegas trip, so I thought you'd better know."

The twins exchanged a look.

"Next month!" the chorused gleefully.

"And why don't we go too?" Adelaide asked Garrett.

As the others broke into several different conversations at once, Frankie glanced at Logan.

"Want to get out of here?" he asked.

"We haven't even eaten yet," she pointed out.

"I know a place that has good dessert."

She eyed him quizzically.

"So we're ditching everyone to go to another restaurant."

A crease appeared between his brows.

"No, not exactly, just… There's something…" He paused, then shook his head. "It's better if I just show you."

He didn't say it, but his eyes were intent, certain. They seemed to be begging her to trust him and Frankie did.

"Would you excommunicate us if we left?" she asked the others as she rose. She knew it didn't matter if if they would. She was only being polite.

"Depends." Garrett's expression was bland as his questioning look went to Logan. "For what reason?"

Frankie cast Logan a sidelong look.

Is Logan flushing?

"I'll explain later," Logan said crisply, rising himself.

"Ooooo," the twins chorused.

"Mysterriioooouuuss," Chance said.

Before they could taunt him anymore, the well-endowed server appeared and the Thatcher boys were distracted by the prospect of food.

"All right suit yourself," Chase muttered. "More wings for us."

Yet before she and Logan turned away, Frankie caught something she knew she wasn't supposed to see—a careful look passed between the others. She froze, a feeling of worry shooting through her. She wanted to demand what they knew that she didn't but she clamped her mouth closed.

Whatever it was, they would have told her if they wanted her to know.

Or maybe that's what this little escape is all about. Logan is going to tell me himself.

Logan slipped his hand into hers as they walked out of the restaurant.

"Sorry about before. You were right. It wasn't the time. Now is."

She gave him a quick hug, relieved that she wasn't going to have to wrench it out of him.

"Good! And you're forgiven…probably."

Logan did a bad job at smiling.

"Guess I'll just have to see."

It didn't take Frankie long to realize that they were going back to the ranch and not another restaurant but she made no comment, not even when they parked and got out of the vehicle.

"What would you say to a night climb?" Logan asked, his gaze beyond her. She bit on her lower lip, remembering the last time they had gone.

"Because last time went so well," Frankie laughed, mistaking his words for a jest.

She paused, then realized he wasn't kidding.

"Oh! You're not joking?" She frowned. "What is up with you anyway? You act all stressed today, deny it, then admit it, then tell me we have to go up a *freaking mountain* in order for you to tell me? Why can't you just tell me right here? And don't tell me it's because you like the night air."

Logan was eyeing her, his expression slightly stupefied.

"I… This is important. It's a surprise."

"Hm."

Frankie let her mind chew on that for a good minute.

Surprises are usually good, aren't they?

Under normal circumstances, Frankie would agree with the thought but Logan was a puzzle all on his own. She often had no idea went on in the layered vastness of that brain of his.

Frankie flung up both arms.

"Fine. But this time I'm texting my sister so they don't send a SWAT team to go find us."

"Fine with me."

Frankie quickly shot off a text and the two started off on

a trail that had now become so familiar and yet so complicated to her.

Complicated like Logan and the way I feel about him.

She and Logan were inseparable, the two almost becoming the same person in so many ways. She reasoned that's why so many of her fears were rooted around him. She was preoccupied with the worry that something would happen to him, to them. She hadn't forgotten how close she'd come to losing him.

"Climbing supplies first," he called back, head already in his trunk as he dug them out.

It only took a minute of walking for the nameless something to settle over Logan again.

"Tell me!" she protested.

"I will," Logan promised.

"Whatever." Frankie shot him an exasperated look. at him. "Can you just tell me why the mountain, of all places? Why if whatever you're telling me is oh-so-important, we have to go there for you to tell me?"

"Why not?" Logan smiled slightly. "It was where both my loves met for the first time."

"Oh, you smooth talker you." Frankie rolled her eyes, though she was smiling. "But if you think this is going to make me drop it…"

Logan shrugged.

"Nah, I know better than that."

Logan's hand in hers felt warm, sturdy and she savored the feeling of his skin against her.

By the time they reached the mountain, Frankie's head felt a bit clearer about Logan, regardless of his heavy mood.

Logan selected an easier climb on this night but the two had been climbing weekly since his recovery and Frankie was surer footed than ever. The night air was cool and laurel scented. They didn't talk as they shimmied up the rocks, but they didn't need to. They were getting there.

Wherever it is we're going.

Only once they reached the ledge did Frankie realize something was off.

"Someone's already been here…" She clambered over the last of the ledge and regarded the Tupperware container. "Left…"

"Dessert," Logan said softly, his eyes full.

And then she understood and she laughed.

He didn't lie. He said he knew a better place for dessert.

He took out the brownie, a mound of fudge that made her mouth water to see and gave her a fork. She sat and began to eat as they Logan opened his mouth to speak.

His voice vibrated with certainty.

"The first time I saw you, I knew. Never had anything like that before – a jolt of pure clarity. For the first time, my life made sense. For the first time, I made sense."

His words resonated inside her and slowly, Frankie put the fork down to stare up at him in wonderment.

"I tried fighting it for a while, it scared me so bad. But we worked out. We work."

Frankie placed the contained on the ledge, her heart swelling.

"You changed things for me, changed the world for me," he was saying now. "Trite, stereotypical, maybe even lame, but it's true. Before, I figured love, belonging, those kinds of things were for other people. Not me."

His eyes closed, as if the words were costing him a physical effort. When they snapped open again, more words came:

"You… you showed me what the world has to offer. And what I have to offer."

His eyes bored directly into her and Frankie felt like he

was seeing her soul, looking at her as if seeing her for the first time.

"You're fun, funny, wild, beautiful, free, everything I didn't even know I wanted, everything I didn't even know could exist in one person."

A shadow passed over his face and when his gaze cut to hers it was with an intensity that scared her, thrilled her. "I've made a lot of mistakes with you, but I don't want not asking you to be my wife to be one of them."

He went quiet then and the words echoed all around Frankie's head.

The first time I saw you I knew... You changed things for me... my wife...

The wind whispered *listen, listen* and the moon had a halo of its own.

Everything was wreathed in perfection, as her mind paused to engrave this scene that she knew she would return to as a touchstone for the rest of her days:

Logan, her man, her one, down on one knee, wearing a new face. It was one she'd never seen before. His eyes narrowed, unflinching, lips set together, jaw at a hopeful tilt, browns pulled slightly up and together. The look was that of pure adulation.

It swirled around her, the memories a timeline, conveyed her up and up until Frankie felt like she was floating, out of her body, marveling down at Logan. Her Logan, so dashing, serious, and gorgeous, with those hazel eyes peering at her, waiting.

He's waiting for an answer!

"Yes, yes of course," she half-laughed, half-sobbed as she jumped to her feet.

She fell back to earth from the heavens, into his arms, his lips, *him*.

There weren't words for this, for the close of his arms

around her. There was no way to describe the rest of his head on hers. It was euphoric and comfortable, exhilarating and safe.

As their chests pressed together, heartbeats thrumming in sync, Frankie thought,

So, this is what love is.

She finally knew where she belonged.

PREVIEW - THE BILLIONAIRE'S HIGH SCHOOL REUNION

SMALL TOWN BILLIONAIRES - BOOK 1

APRIL MURDOCK

Have you read the first book in the Small Town Billionaires Series?

Here's a preview in case you missed the series.

Want to skip the preview and go straight to Amazon to get it? Here's the link:

https://amzn.to/2GZcXYT

CHAPTER 1

"Is this the place?"

Blake Murphy glanced over at his best friend Travis, who was driving their rental car. Travis raised a single eyebrow at him, gesturing to the building in front of them, prompting Blake to answer his question. Outside, the bright Arizona sun was beating down, a noticeable contrast to the dread that was building in Blake's stomach.

"Yeah," Blake said, clearing his throat while looking at the building.

It was one story, built of plain tan bricks and sprawling over yellowing grass. Afton Bluff High School had never been very impressive, and this was something Blake had known even when he had attended school there, but he felt a rush of school pride even though he hated to admit it. Though he wasn't looking forward to being back here, he was reliving every ride back to the school after football games, every homecoming parade, and every team huddle.

They parked and Travis let out a low whistle as they got out of the car. Blake rolled his eyes at him, rethinking his decision to bring him along. It had been years since Blake had been home, always opting to have his parents travel out to his place in LA for holidays, rather than returning to Arizona. The town held nothing for him but regret, and every time the high school called him, asking if he could speak at graduation or open the football season, he always came up with a reason that he couldn't make it.

Not that it was hard to find them - he was a busy man, running his own company and co-hosting a talk show on ESPN with Travis, who was nothing short of a handful. Blake didn't know how Elise, his wife, could stand to deal with him. Every. Single. Day. The woman was a saint.

"She's a beauty," Travis said, laughing as they got closer to the building. Blake rolled his eyes but couldn't help cracking a smile at his friend's sarcasm. Travis turned to him, raising his arms and spinning in front of the door. "Does every high school look the same?"

"Probably. At least they all feel the same. Full of angst, memories, and hormones," Blake laughed, even as the nervous knot in his stomach was increasing in size. They stepped through the door and a wave of nostalgia washed over him so strongly he had to close his eyes and take a breath. He hadn't wanted to come back. It was only at the urging of Travis and the others at the show that he finally made the decision to get on the flight and spend a week in his hometown. A whole week. Ugh.

Blake could still remember the day he had gotten the call - his assistant had answered the phone while they were in the studio, saying someone was inviting him to come back to town for his ten-year high school reunion. Blake had immediately waved him off, telling him to inform the person on the phone that he had an event planned and wouldn't be able to make it.

Travis had punched him in the shoulder, scowling at him much the way he did when they had differing opinions about something happening in the league. Blake had seen that look during the last draft, and he knew it meant Travis was going to stop at nothing to bring Blake around to his way of thinking.

"Hey man, those are your peeps! You gotta go back to them, remember where you came from! You know, roots and all." Travis was emphatic, banging his fist on the table and meeting Blake's eyes solidly, his filled with conviction.

"I see my people plenty enough," Blake had replied, hoping Travis would just drop it and move on. "My parents are here all the time. You know that."

"Your parents aren't your only people." Travis had said back, launching them into a full discussion about Blake's hometown that eventually led him to confess the reason he didn't want to come back for the high school reunion, and the reason he hadn't gone back for the five-year reunion, either.

Trista Kennedy.

Blake hated thinking about her, and he hated thinking about how he had ruined his chance with the only girl he had really ever loved. She was probably married by now, living a nice happy life with a man who had been there for her. A man who listened to her and supported her dreams.

"So you've made some mistakes," Travis had said, hounding him just about every time they had come into the studio together. "It's never too late to fix them."

"No, Travis," Blake had said back, trying not to meet the other man's eyes. "Sometimes it *is* too late."

No matter how many times Blake told Travis that it was too late for him to go back and patch things up with Trista, he persisted, telling him that life was nothing without second chances. Though Blake had tried to hold out and ignore him, Travis had won in the end, and that's why they were walking through the lobby of the school building, the smell bringing back unpleasant memories for Blake.

"Hey, man!" Travis said, stopping and pointing to a plaque in the trophy case. Blake cringed as Travis pointed to a plaque and a trophy with Blake's name inscribed, a picture of the eighteen-year-old him standing with his arms crossed in his football jersey.

BLAKE 'BOMBER' MURPHY

"That's cool, man, I didn't know they called you that in high school, too," Travis said. Bomber had been Blake's nickname because of his ability to throw long passes. Trista had been the one to give him the name after a homecoming game junior year. He'd thrown two long passes that had both been caught for touchdowns. What a game that had been!

Blake cleared his throat, feeling more uneasy. It seemed as though everything in the high school reminded him of her. Even his own name!

"Yeah," he said, looking away from it, turning toward the hallway he knew they were going to have to walk down to get to the gym, which is where they were supposed to meet to help set up for the reunion. With every step he took, he was regretting his decision more and more. The thought of seeing Trista again, who no doubt was helping with the reunion, was driving his anxiety.

Why had he agreed to help set up? If he was going to come back for this thing, he should have just come for the get-together and let that be it. But no, he'd allowed himself to be coerced into doing this by his good friend and near enemy, Travis Bennett.

He and Travis walked into the gym and as soon as he saw her, Blake felt a wave of guilt and longing crash over him.

Trista turned around, a string of lights in her hand. He caught her forget-me-not blue eyes and took a sharp breath, trying to remember the last time he'd had the chance to look into them. Trista had frozen in her spot on the ladder, staring back at him.

Several other people were in the gym, all people who Blake recognized immediately. It was weird to see people so long after graduation - it was still them, but slightly different. A little older. A little more confident.

"Well," someone said in a haughty voice. "Look who *finally* decided to show up. We started setting up for the reunion *yesterday*."

Blake looked over at Quentin Lee, who hadn't changed much since they had graduated high school. He still had stark black hair and black eyes, and a permanent expression like he knew he could do whatever it was that you were doing, but better. He also had a nasty habit of stressing too many words when he spoke, which made him sound overly serious. Blake bit his tongue to hold his temper in check, because all during high school he had wanted to bite back at him, but he never had.

"Hey, my bad. I couldn't get away till today," Travis said, in the way he did when he noticed tension and was doing his best to ease it. "What's important is that we're here now, and we're ready to party. Hey, man, you want to introduce me to your old classmates?" Travis looked over at Blake and nodded his head to get Blake to settle down.

Blake swallowed, nodded, and looked back at the other people in the gym, trying to gather some of the courage he had when he was getting in front of the camera, ready to share his opinion with the world. In the years since he had started his talk show, he had found that it had become easier to talk to people, but now, standing in front of his old classmates, he was finding it hard to get out a word.

"This is Quentin Lee," Blake started, clearing his throat again and gesturing to the him. "And this is Leslie Fay."

Travis shook hands with Quentin and a blonde woman stepped out from her place at Trista's ladder. Her eyes were quick and suspicious, and though she shook Travis's hand, she looked as though she didn't particularly enjoy it.

"Travis Bennett. Blake and I work together." Though their history was far more than simple work pals, Travis chose to leave it at that. Blake realized he'd been rude for not introducing him and he'd had to do it himself. He was grateful for Travis' brevity given the oversight. He must be taking pity since normally he'd pay a higher price for forgetting the introduction.

Blake swallowed through the lump in his throat as Leslie's gaze swung to him, and she narrowed her eyes even further.

Leslie had gone to high school with them, but she and Trista hadn't been good friends back then. Blake wondered briefly if they were friends now. If so, that would mean Leslie had likely heard all about the details of their relationship and break up. Blake took in a deep breath and let it out slowly, then introduced a few of the other people standing around the gym. Travis shook hands with each one.

"And this is Trista Kennedy," Blake said, giving Trista a small smile and gesturing to her. She smiled politely at he and Travis, but there was something in her eyes that Blake couldn't quite read. He wished he could go back to the time when he always knew what she was thinking.

"Valedictorian," Quentin said, finishing Blake's introduction. "And organizer for the reunion."

Travis raised his eyebrows at Blake, looking between Quentin and Trista curiously. Trista smiled, but turned around and started focusing on hanging her lights again, rather than contributing to the conversation.

After the introductions, Blake turned his attention to the

state of the gym. Though Quentin had said that they had been at work since the day before, the gym looked shabby and sad. Blake met Travis's eyes and he had to stifle a laugh at the dusty, drooping decorations. Behind them, Trista had finished hanging their lights, but found that after Quentin plugged them in for her, only half of the string actually lit up.

Trista climbed down the ladder, frustration clear on her face.

"Alright," Travis said, clapping his hands and looking to her. "What can we do to help? What else needs to be done? I probably won't know what to do on my own, but I can follow instructions."

"Well," Trista said, sighing and putting a hand up to massage her temple, "there isn't really much more we can do... We're light on decorations to begin with, and what we do have doesn't even work. We've already hung most of the streamers and balloons. I suppose you guys could help set up tables and chairs."

Travis and Blake followed as Trista instructed them on where to put the tables, and Quentin and Leslie stopped what they were doing to help, both watching the two newcomers closely. Blake had never felt so studied in his life, and he'd played pro football and now had a career in television.

"Oh, sorry," he said, turning around with a chair and nearly running Trista over. She took a few steps back and met his eyes, and he felt as though someone had punched him in the gut.

"That's okay," she said, laughing and quickly averting her eyes from his. "I should watch where I'm going."

Blake felt guilt heavily in the pit of his stomach, but continued to work, running into Trista or accidentally meeting her eyes again and again as the tables and chairs slowly got put into place.

Travis gave Blake a look when they had finished setting up the tables, and Blake glanced over to see Trista shaking her head and looking distraught. He took this as a moment to really see her again - though she had always been curvy, those curves had softened since they were in high school. She was beautiful still, with long sable brown hair that fell in loose curls around her shoulders.

Blake remembered running his hands through those curls, and he remembered cupping her face in his hands and kissing her. Knowing he should refocus away from these memories, he wished desperately that he could kiss her again. Something in his chest ached for her as he watched her look around the gym in dismay.

"Trista, do we have another extension cord somewhere? And what happened to the banner that was supposed to go over the front door?" Leslie was holding yet another string of lights that looked worn out.

"There should be another cord, at least I thought there was…" Trista said, rubbing her forehead and looking around. She sighed and looked up at the ceiling. "There is no budget for this thing! It's like they expect us to pull off a reunion party with nothing."

Travis elbowed Blake in the side and Blake raised his eyebrows at him, not knowing what he meant. Travis rolled his eyes as Leslie asked for their help stringing up more lights, and the two men walked away from Trista to help. Travis gave Blake a meaningful look but Blake looked away, not wanting to acknowledge the fact that since they'd arrived this morning, Blake had been drawn to Trista.

"Okay, guys," Trista said, about an hour later. "Let's call it a night. I'm going to raid the shed out behind the football field tomorrow morning to see if I can find anything else we might be able to use to make this better." Trista met Blake's eyes briefly, then her eyes quickly cut away. "Good night, everybody."

∽

Want to find out what happens next? Get your copy of *The Billionaire's High School Reunion* on Amazon

https://amzn.to/2GZcXYT

∽

WANT A FREE BOOK?

If you enjoyed this sweet billionaire romance, I'd love to give you another one for free! Join my readers group and you'll receive a copy of *The Billionaire's First Love* as my gift to you.

∽

Jack's back home after eight years away. Tracie isn't prepared to see him again. When she does, she realizes he still has her heart. They'd started out as best friends and even then she loved him. Can they pick up where they left off? Is life that simple? Is love ever that easy?

∽

Tap here to get your copy of *The Billionaire's First Love*

https://dl.bookfunnel.com/ssfn7ng99x

ABOUT APRIL MURDOCK

April Murdock loves romance, especially sweet stories that make you sigh out loud. She loves to write stories inspired by people in her life – past and present. Okay, so truthfully, she's never known a billionaire or anyone from royal bloodlines, but taking reality and pumping it up a bit is what makes it fun!

April has lived her whole life in the Southern US. Traveling is a great love, but coming home to Georgia where her heart is makes her happy. April is married to her high school sweetheart. Their children are married and they can't wait to have grandchildren to spoil.

~

Connect With April on Facebook

April's Website

~

Made in the USA
Middletown, DE
06 July 2020